Murder in the Museum

Murder in the Museum

John Rowland

With an Introduction
by Martin Edwards

Poisoned Pen Press

Originally published in London in 1938 by Herbert Jenkins
Copyright © 2016 Estate of John Rowland
Introduction Copyright © 2016 Martin Edwards

Published by Poisoned Pen Press in association with the
British Library

First Edition 2016
First US Trade Paperback Edition

10 9 8 7 6 5 4 3 2 1

Library of Congress Catalog Card Number: 2015949196

ISBN: 9781464205798   Trade Paperback

Poisoned Pen Press
6962 E. First Ave., Ste. 103
Scottsdale, AZ 85251
www.poisonedpenpress.com
info@poisonedpenpress.com

Printed in the United States of America

Contents

Introduction

It is perhaps appropriate that the British Library should republish John Rowland's *Murder in the Museum*, which made its first appearance in 1938. At the time that Rowland's book came out, the United Kingdom's national library formed part of the British Museum, which in this book supplies a memorable crime scene.

Meek, mild-mannered Henry Fairhurst is undertaking research in the domed reading room at the Museum. "An assiduous reader of detective stories", he indulges in idle speculation about his fellow occupants of the reading room. One red-haired individual who catches his eye appears to be asleep, but when Henry approaches him, he discovers that the man is dead. He has been poisoned with cyanide.

Inspector Shelley, who featured in most of Rowland's detective novels, takes charge of the inquiry, but Henry finds himself fascinated by the case, and strives to remain involved. Shelley is an affable fellow, and—as in several other John Rowland books—he proves willing to allow an amateur to assist with the investigation, generosity that may be surprising but tends to justify itself with results.

This combination of professional and amateur detectives, whether working side-by-side or as rivals, was not unusual in crime fiction of the 1930s. Henry Fairhurst is reminiscent of

Ambrose Chitterwick, who featured in three excellent novels written by Anthony Berkeley, one of the most influential crime novelists of the era. Chitterwick, like Henry, is hen-pecked, and is subservient to a domineering aunt, much as Henry is bossed around by his formidable sister. The simi-larities are particularly apparent when one compares this book to Berkeley's *The Piccadilly Murder*, a cleverly contrived mystery which opens with Chitterwick witnessing a murder by cyanide whilst taking tea in a London hotel.

John Rowland was not an innovator, like Berkeley, but this novel is typical of many which appeared during the 1930s. One aspect of this book which calls for comment is the presentation of a character who happens to be Jewish. Readers will appreciate that some of the language used would not be regarded as appropriate in a novel written today, because of an element of stereotyping. The British Library has given careful thought to this issue, but concluded that, on balance, it was right to present the text as originally written. It seems abundantly clear from the context that Rowland had no intention to be offensive towards Jewish people—quite the contrary—and modern readers will at least gain an understanding of attitudes and language that were the norm at the time this book was written, and which would be sacrificed by an attempt to impose twenty-first century editorial values.

Very little has previously been written about John Row-land. Thanks to information kindly supplied by his son Fytton, I am glad to be able to cast more light on the life of this long-neglected writer. John Herbert Shelley Rowland was born in Bodmin, Cornwall, in 1907, the son of a grocer. John was a traditional name in his family, Herbert was his own father's first name, and Shelley was his mother's maiden name. Rowland gave the latter name to his fictional detec-tive, Inspector Henry Shelley.

After attending Bodmin Grammar School, and the sixth form at Plymouth College, Rowland read chemistry at Bristol University. A lower second class degree did not enable him to pursue a career in research, so he trained as a teacher, and in 1930 went to teach science at the Prior's School in Lifford, County Donegal. His long-term ambition, however, was always to be a writer, and after a couple of years he moved to London, securing an editorial job with Charles Watts—to whom *Murder in the Museum* is dedicated.

Watts was involved with the Rationalist movement (now called humanism) and some of Rowland's duties concerned running the Rationalist Press. He started to write his own detective stories in his spare time, and they were published by the firm of Herbert Jenkins. While in London, he socialised in literary circles, and his author friends included L.A.G. Strong, M.P. Shiel, and even Dylan Thomas. None of them were primarily associated with detective fiction, but Strong and Shiel dabbled in the genre, while Thomas co-wrote a spoof of the detective story that was not published until after his death. Rowland also became a close friend of the poet John Gawsworth (a pseudonym of Terence Ian Fytton Armstrong).

In 1937, Rowland married a nurse from Yorkshire, Gertrude Adams. When the Second World War started, he was conscripted into the scientific civil service instead of the armed forces, because he had a degree in chemistry. He worked in the management of armaments factories, initially at Woolwich Arsenal and later at various places around the country (including Thorp Arch, on the site of which the British Library's branch at Boston Spa now stands). The Rowlands' only child was born in 1944, and given one of Gawsworth's middle names, Fytton.

After the war ended, Rowland resumed working for Watts, and publishing detective stories. By 1950 he felt secure enough to resign from his day job, becoming a free-lance writer. The family moved to Leeds, where they stayed for two years. In Leeds, however, Rowland's religious views underwent a fundamental change. Influenced by a Unitarian minister called Reginald Wilde, he abandoned humanism, and became a Unitarian. Not content with that, he resolved to become a Unitarian minister himself, and in 1952 he was appointed lay pastor in charge of the Unitarian church in Brighton. For several years he commuted from Brighton to attend Manchester College, Oxford, to train for the ministry. During this period he had little time to spare for writing, although after qualifying as a minister, he started writing again.

Reading tastes had changed, however, and Rowland was unable to find a market for detective stories of the kind he preferred. He decided to concentrate on non-fiction, and specifically on criminology and biographies of scientists and technologists aimed at teenagers. He also became the editor of a magazine called *The Unitarian*. His output declined gradually in quantity, but right up to his death he was a "stringer" covering the village in which he lived for the local weekly newspaper. He always gave his profession as "journalist" rather than "writer".

Gertrude died in 1967, and Rowland later married Marguerite Miller, a widowed member of his congregation. His final church was in Trowbridge, Wiltshire, and he retired to Somerset, dying in 1984 at the age of 76. By that time, his detective novels had been forgotten, but thanks to the British Library's Crime Classics series, readers now have the opportunity to rediscover them.

Martin Edwards

www.martinedwardsbooks.com

Chapter I

Death!

Beneath the high, gloomy dome, Henry Fairhurst looked around him. There was an air of deathly stillness in the place, and a silence broken only by the occasional rustle of pages and the subdued murmur of a borrower discussing books with an official. The British Museum Reading Room is a strange place, and Henry Fairhurst had not been within its privileged precincts for many a long day, but he had now managed to get hold of some literary research on behalf of an enterprising journalist who was contemplating the writing of a life of an obscure French courtesan in the seventeenth century.

Mr. Fairhurst did not see anything strange in the fact that he—the most respectable native of respectable Streatham—should be investigating the scandalous doings of the Paris *demi-monde* of three hundred years before. If his sister, who kept house for him, had uttered the word "mistress" in his hearing (save, of course, as applied to a lady who makes servants obey her whims) he would have blushed. Yet, without a blush or even a blench, he read the books of old-fashioned

French historians in an age when the conventions were not as rigid as now.

It was, he thought, adjusting his gold-rimmed pince-nez on his ridiculous little turned-up nose, pleasant to be back in the good old "B.M." once again. He breathed in the somewhat viscous air with real joy, and made his way to the central tables or desks (he could never quite make up his mind which word was most appropriate) where the catalogues were arranged, and hunted for some of the books he wanted to read for his note-taking purposes. Then, having placed his bowler hat and umbrella on a table to keep his place, he filled out some forms, made his way back to the place which he had reserved, and waited in as good patience as he could command for the books to arrive. (It is, one would like to point out, one of the few drawbacks to working in the British Museum that all the books one wishes to use are always so far away that the willing assistants take a matter of half an hour or so to procure them.)

Henry did not really mind the wait. He had a little game which he used to amuse himself by playing in idle moments. What Sarah, his spinster sister, would have said had she known of this little propensity of his, it is not easy to imagine. But she did not know—so what matter? This little pastime of Henry's was what he was pleased to call the "Sherlock Holmes" game. He would look earnestly at someone who was sitting opposite him in a bus or train, and would try to decide what that person's occupation in life was likely to be. He had not the satisfaction of knowing if his diagnosis was ever correct, but he had the mental joy of a secret occupation.

The British Museum Reading Room was an ideal place for such an occupation, as its inhabitants were so pleasantly variegated. Henry adjusted his pince-nez again, anticipating some sport. That tough-looking specimen over there, now.

What could he be? "Confidence-man," Henry murmured to himself, unconsciously libelling a University Professor, who was the world's greatest expert on lepidoptera.

The grey-haired, elderly negro sitting next to him was not a suitable subject for Henry's little game, as it did not need the brains of a Sherlock Holmes to deduce his profession from his clerical collar.

On the next chair, however, sitting with his head lolling back in an attitude of complete abandonment, was a specimen of the most remarkable interest. (Henry always thought of the subject of his perverted detective genius as a "specimen.") This man had flaming red hair of the colour known to rude little schoolboys as "carroty." He wore a pair of enormous horn-rimmed spectacles, and his chin, though technically clean shaven, had not been touched by a razor for several days. Yet his clothes, though stained with egg and with the remnants of other meals, were well cut, and had obviously been purchased from a good tailor in the West End of London. And as he lay back, his enormous cavern of a mouth half open, Henry caught a glimpse of gold teeth. Obviously a man of some money, then, though equally obviously caring but little of his appearance. His collar was dirty and his tie askew—so terrifyingly askew that Henry thought it the first time he had ever seen a tie literally worn under the ear.

And then, in the sacred precincts of the British Museum Reading Room, a strange sound smote Henry's ear. What could it be? Surely it couldn't be…surely it couldn't be…Yes; it was a veritable snore! It was, not to put too fine a point on it, a snore of the most gargantuan proportions, and it was being emitted by the large red-haired gentleman on whose precise position in society Henry had just been speculating.

Henry had summed him up as a *nouveau-riche*—probably a millionaire with a bee in his bonnet, perhaps writing a book to prove that Queen Victoria had written Shakespeare's plays, or something equally crazy. It seemed impossible to connect such an uncouth individual with any sort of interest in abstract knowledge of something like a rational kind.

And now this snore. What could be the meaning of it? Henry was never one to accept the obvious explanation, and he could not believe that what he found to be the exciting atmosphere of the Reading Room could possibly bore anyone so much as to send him to sleep. No. There must be some other, some less obvious explanation.

Suddenly Henry sat bolt upright in his chair. He had always been an assiduous reader of detective stories, and now he thought that he had hit upon the explanation of the snores, which were still ascending in a mighty crescendo, in spite of the titters and scowls with which they were being greeted.

This would never do. Perhaps the man had been drugged by a gang of crooks. Perhaps they were even now robbing his house, knowing that they had rendered him helpless for a period of hours. Perhaps they were kidnapping his beautiful daughter, with a view to holding her to ransom. Perhaps... (It is possibly unnecessary to add that Henry's detective-story reading was usually to be found in the more bloodthirsty shelves of the local lending library.)

Henry, although he was small, and although his pince-nez, his bowler hat, his umbrella, his blue serge suit, and his spats might suggest timid respectability, was no coward. While the rest of the inhabitants of the Reading Room sat around and either smiled or frowned at the snores, according as the work on which they were engaged was interesting or the reverse, Henry made up his mind that something must be done about this man. After all, he might be a lunatic with some crazy hair-brained scheme in his mind, but it would doubtless embarrass him considerably if he were found in such a position, a centre of mingled wrath and amusement in the world's most famous library.

Rising to his feet slowly, Henry made his way over to the man. The snores had subsided now. They must have lasted some two or three minutes, almost without ceasing, and now the man was merely breathing heavily, and even that seemed to die down as Henry approached him. However, his eyes were still tightly closed and his mouth was wide open.

Henry grasped the man's shoulder firmly. "Look here, old man, this won't do," he said with forced affability.

There was no response. The man was still as a rock. Not a movement could Henry see in his face. It was all very mystifying, very curious. Henry could not understand it at all. He was completely puzzled by it.

Mastering his repugnance, he grasped the man's shoulder even more firmly and gave him a brisk shake. "Wake up!" he said, quite loudly.

Slowly, like a water-logged boat sinking under the waves, the man's head rolled round on his shoulders. He lolled forward, his head on the table, and then, his knees sagging and giving way beneath him, he slipped under the table on to the floor.

Henry rapidly knelt beside him, and grasped his wrist. Then he looked around in amazement. The whole room swam before his eyes, because the man who had been snoring so stertorously a few minutes before was now so very quiet, so very still. There was no movement anywhere in his great frame. There was no trace of a pulse. The man was dead!

Chapter II

Cross-Examination

"Now, Mr. Fairhurst." Inspector Shelley looked sternly at the little man, as if he did not quite understand what such a mild specimen of humanity could possibly be doing in such a mysterious affair.

"Yes, Inspector." Henry looked at the Scotland Yard man, deeply impressed that at last he was meeting one of the great men of whose work he had so often read in the papers. He peered over his pince-nez and positively purred with satisfaction. This, indeed, was something to tell Sarah about!

"I want you," the Inspector went on, "to tell me precisely what happened, to explain how the man came to die, what attracted your attention, and why you walked over to him just at the moment of his death."

Henry shuddered. "To tell you the truth, Inspector," he said, "I hardly know."

"But you must have some sort of idea, surely."

"A vague idea, anyhow," contributed Sergeant Cunningham, who had accompanied his chief on this errand of investigation, but who had hitherto remained silent.

Henry giggled. It is regrettable to admit the fact, but he was the type of man who would giggle on occasion.

"Well, gentlemen," he said. "I am one of those strange people—the students of humanity. The dead man attracted my attention because he was, if I may say so, of such a striking and unusual appearance. I found myself watching him almost unconsciously, in the way that one sometimes does watch a stranger who strikes one, if you understand me."

"I understand you, Mr. Fairhurst," said Shelley in sympathetic tones, "but I still want answers to a few other questions, you know."

"Fire away, Inspector," Henry answered, and then, conscious that this piece of slang was somewhat undignified for a man of his position in the social world of Streatham, he added: "Or, if I might borrow a word from the gangster films, I would say, 'Shoot!'"

"First of all," remarked Shelley briskly, "did you see anyone else approach the man in the last few minutes before he died?"

Henry reflected. "I have a sort of vague notion that someone was walking away from the man as I approached," he admitted. "It's only the vaguest of impressions, though, and I couldn't possibly swear to it for a moment."

"Was it a man or a woman?" asked Cunningham, with a glance of apology at his chief. "Will your memory give you any information on that point, Mr. Fairhurst?"

Again Henry reflected deeply for a moment before replying.

"It's difficult," he murmured. "You see, I may be getting some quite innocent person into trouble if I..."

"Don't worry about that," Shelley interrupted. "If any innocent person is involved in this case we shall clear him without the slightest difficulty. Don't worry about that for a moment, Mr. Fairhurst."

"Well," Henry admitted somewhat unwillingly, "I must say that I have an idea that a woman had been talking to the man before he died. But I couldn't swear to it. You see, there are so many people in that Reading Room that it might easily be a mistake on my part. Some perfect stranger might trip over the man's chair, and pause to apologise. That might easily account for the fact that I thought a woman was talking to the man. Or," he concluded somewhat lamely, "there may not have been any one there at all."

"Got that, Cunningham?" asked Shelley. His assistant nodded.

"Only one thing, sir," he added.

"Yes?" Shelley was always prepared to take a hint of a useful line of investigation.

"Do you think Mr. Fairhurst could be induced to remember the sort of clothes the lady was dressed in?"

Henry looked from one detective to the other with some surprise. What on earth would these men ask next? How did they expect him to remember the attire of a lady of whose very existence he was not certain?

Yet he found himself answering. "I have a definite impression of a youngish lady, rather pretty, and dressed in some sort of dark jumper and skirt," he said. "Further than that I'm afraid I cannot go."

"Very useful, Mr. Fairhurst," was Shelley's comment. "Very useful indeed. I expect we'll lay our hands on that young lady before many hours are past; then maybe we shall be wiser than we are now on the subject of Arnell's death."

"Arnell?" Henry's tone was interrogative.

"Oh, yes." Shelley smiled, and his smile transformed that somewhat grim face, with its eyes of steel grey, into a new countenance, friendly and inviting confidences—a deceptive change that had, in its time, been the undoing of many a criminal.

"Professor Julius Arnell," he went on. "That's the fellow's name. Does it mean anything to you?"

"I know his work, of course," said Henry.

"What sort of work?" Shelley could be crisp enough in his utterance when he felt himself to be on the track of some useful information.

"He was probably the world's greatest authority on the minor Elizabethans," said Henry. "He had written many books on the lesser dramatists of that time, and he was, I believe, Professor of English Literature at one of the provincial universities. I never remember seeing him in the Reading Room before, however. Possibly he was able to come up only now and then. I expect he had to do a good deal of lecturing in connection with his post at Portavon—yes, that's where he was—as they usually work their staff pretty hard in those places."

"Did he have any enemies?" Shelley whipped the question out, like a rifle bullet.

Henry smiled. "I didn't know him at all, Inspector," he said. "He may have had hundreds of enemies in his private life, for all I know. All that I can tell you is that he was pretty cordially hated in the world of literary research."

"Why?"

"Isn't it obvious enough?"

"I don't think it is. Explain yourself, my dear fellow." Shelley's temper was even enough, but he was beginning to find the little man's finicky correctness more than a little trying.

"When a man reaches the position of being a leading authority on any subject," Henry explained patiently, "he cannot say much on the subject of his speciality without treading on someone's corns. You see?"

Shelley nodded. "I see," he said. "And you think that Arnell may have been murdered by someone who loathed him because he had a bit of a nasty temper in matters of literary research and so on."

"Oh, no!" Henry pushed the idea away from him, horror expressed in every line of his meek little face. "I did not suggest anything of the sort, Inspector. I did not mean you to infer anything at all like that. Please don't read into my words more than I say."

"Right ho, Mr. Fairhurst," Shelley agreed with heavy joviality. "And who were the other experts in this business of the lesser Elizabethan dramatists—which, I think you said, was Arnell's speciality?"

"That's not easy to say," answered Henry, seeing only too clearly whither this cross-examination was leading, and mentally viewing himself as the principal witness for the crown in a case against one University Professor for the murder of another one. "You might ask," he went on, unhappily, "Professor Wilkinson of Northfield University, and Dr. Crocker, who is, I think, in some sort of official position, of Oxford—as far as I know, they were the only two who knew much about the work which Arnell had done—I've heard them discussing things together at meetings of learned societies, and so on, which I have occasionally attended."

"Thank you, Mr. Fairhurst," said Shelley appreciatively. "You have been very useful to us. If you will hold yourself in readiness for the inquest, I think that we have finished with you for the moment."

"But don't you…don't you…" Henry stuttered and dithered in his eagerness to get the question out.

"Don't we what?" asked Shelley ungrammatically.

"Don't you want to hear how he died?"

"We know that," answered the detective with a smile. "He apparently went off to sleep, breathed stertorously for a few minutes—possibly so loudly as to seem to be snoring—and then collapsed."

"But how do you know?" asked Henry.

Shelley smiled again. "We have our methods, Mr. Fairhurst," he said. There was no doubt that Inspector Shelley could on occasion be a very trying man.

When Henry had departed with his exciting news with which to enliven the somewhat sleepy dovecots of Streatham, Cunningham looked at his chief. They were comfortably ensconced in a small room at the Museum, nominally the abode, during hours, of a library assistant.

"Sure you're right, chief?" he murmured.

"Absolutely." Shelley could be very resolute when he chose. "The man died of cyanide poisoning. His lips smelled of almonds when we examined him. And he must have had a pretty hefty dose of cyanide to pop off as quickly as that, without regaining consciousness."

"Accident or suicide?"

"Accident can, I think, be ruled out. Suicide is just possible, of course," Shelley admitted. "It's not at all likely, though."

"Why not?"

"Two reasons," said Shelley succinctly. "One: because it is not really likely that such a man as Arnell, a respected figure in the academic world, would commit suicide in the full view of the public. After all, I do know a little about these university people. I've been among them before. And they are in many ways different from us merely ordinary folk. Anyhow, I think, if Arnell wanted to commit suicide, he would do so in the decent privacy of his own home, so that there was at any rate a possibility that he would be thought to have died in his bed—of heart failure, say. It all comes down to a matter of psychology, really."

Shelley's liking for the somewhat high-falutin jargon of the psychologists was well-known at Scotland Yard, and Cunningham, having no desire to listen to a lecture on the comparative merits of Freud, Jung, and Adler, hastened to turn his chief off this track of surmise on to something more likely to be immediately profitable.

"And reason number two?" he asked.

"These," said Shelley, producing a packet of sweets.

"Sugared almonds," murmured Cunningham. "Interesting."

"Very interesting indeed, and very suggestive," said Shelley.

"Why suggestive?" Cunningham knew that Shelley found this sort of talk valuable. To argue out any case to a sympathetic listener was always helpful.

Shelley smiled at the naive question. "You understand my funny ways, oh my Cunningham," he said. "I've no doubt that you really know about all these things as much as I know myself. But I won't apologise for pursuing the obvious, as it does make things easier to work them out in words. These almonds are suggestive, because I feel pretty sure that they are the way in which the poison was given."

Cunningham's face expressed such a feeling of complete incredulity that Shelley laughed aloud.

"Consider, Cunningham," he said. "Cyanide has a distinct almond flavour. If some of it were placed inside a sweet of this kind, would the recipient of it know that fact?"

"Well," said Cunningham thoughtfully. "I wouldn't say that it wouldn't be tasted."

"If he chewed it up," said Shelley, "it would be obvious enough that there was something queer about the sweet. But he would attribute it to something wrong with the making of the thing, and would probably want to spit it out and throw it away. But before he had time to do that the cyanide would be in his system. He would be sleeping his last sleep before the thought of poison really had time to penetrate his mind."

"Think so?" Cunningham was still mildly incredulous.

"Certain." Shelley was emphatic. "I'm perfectly sure that Professor Arnell was fond of almonds, that some person at present unknown was aware of his little weakness, and that he was given a good hefty dose of cyanide in an almond. There's the crime in a nutshell. Whether that person unknown is Mr. Fairhurst's mysterious young lady is the thing that we have first to find out. But meanwhile let's see what we can find about the late Professor Arnell from the reference books."

He touched a bell on the table, and an assistant came silently in. "Can you get me a copy of *Who's Who*, and the Royal Literary Society's *Handbook*?" asked Shelley. In a minute or less the books were before them.

Shelley rapidly scanned the correct pages of the reference books, and made rapid notes.

"Well, sir?" asked Cunningham.

"Professor Arnell lived at Pinner," said Shelley. "He was Professor Emeritus at Portavon—in other words, he had retired from active life—and he apparently lived with his daughter. Query, Cunningham: is Miss Arnell the mysterious lady seen by our Mr. Fairhurst?"

"Any other pointers?"

"There may be more in this case than meets the eye, Cunningham," said Shelley.

"Why?"

"Do you remember Arnell, the oil millionaire? Owned half of the State of Texas, then sold out, and came to England to live twenty or thirty years ago?"

"The name seems familiar to me in some way," Cunningham admitted.

"He died two years ago," said Shelley. "I remember the report in the papers quite clearly."

"But what's that to do with this case, sir?" asked Cunningham.

"A lot," said Shelley crisply. "He was Professor Arnell's father."

"Yes?" The question was implied in Cunningham's intonation.

"When a millionaire dies in mysterious circumstances," said Shelley, "look for the money motives, Cunningham."

"And what are the money motives here?"

"That's what we have to find out," said Shelley.

But it was to be a long time before they disentangled the web of mystery. And in the meantime Henry Fairhurst was doing his bit.

Chapter III

Henry at Home

"Really, Henry, I do think this is most unreasonable of you."

Miss Sarah Fairhurst was as aggressive as her younger brother was the reverse. Tall, with penetrating blue eyes, and with greying hair tightly brushed back from a high, narrow forehead, she was the type of born spinster who nevertheless succeeds in lording it over the rest of mankind by sheer persistent unpleasantness.

"Why unreasonable?" asked Henry uneasily. He saw yet another squabble on the emotional horizon, and he had the mild man's habitual dislike of squabbles.

"You distinctly promised me," she said, "that you would be home to tea today. Quite distinctly, Henry. But there—when you get up in the West End with those disreputable literary friends of yours, what does your poor, lonely sister matter? Heaven knows what you do with yourself." Miss Fairhurst's tone hinted at unspeakable orgies.

"Still," she continued, "if you do manage to get some work done which keeps us supplied in food, I suppose I must not grumble too much. Although I do think that, if there is any likelihood of your meeting some of your dreadful friends, you might do your best to let me know beforehand, so that the tea does not spoil in the pot while I wait endless hours for you."

Rapidly Henry seized the olive-branch that was held out to him.

"As a matter of fact, my dear," he said mildly, "I couldn't help being late today."

"No? What was it this time? A blonde or a brunette?" It was an accepted fiction with Miss Fairhurst that her brother spent all his leisure hours in the arms of attractive ladies with all the charms that she lacked.

"Neither. It was an inspector from Scotland Yard," Henry explained.

"Scotland Yard. Rubbish!" exclaimed his sister emphatically. "What would Scotland Yard want with you? They only look after criminals, and with all your faults I have never suspected you of crime, my dear Henry, and neither, I am sure, has anyone else."

"I am not a criminal, Sarah," explained Henry with what he privately considered an air of quiet dignity, "but I was a witness to a crime—I was, as far as I can see, the sole witness to a murder."

"Murder! Sole witness! My dear Henry, you'll be getting all our throats cut in our beds." Miss Fairhurst somehow contrived to give the impression that if her brother had become involved in such a disgraceful affair it was all his fault and would bring disgrace upon the house.

"The man died in the Reading Room at the British Museum," Henry explained patiently, but his sister at first would have nothing of it.

"Don't talk nonsense," she said brusquely. "Drink your tea and don't go dithering about things that you don't understand."

"All right," said Henry, and did as he was told—as, to tell the truth, he always did with this formidable sister who had ordered him about since childhood, and who would apparently always continue to do so.

For a few minutes tea continued in silence. Then Sarah spoke again.

"A man died in the Reading Room," she said. "Wasn't there another case like that a few months ago?"

"Another case?"

"Yes. Some lecturer or professor of something," answered Miss Fairhurst vaguely. "I seem to remember reading about it. In the papers, you know, though of course one realises that they tell the most dreadful lies, and one can never be at all sure of the facts of the case."

"Are you certain?" Henry put down his cup and gazed at his sister, fairly trembling with eagerness. "Can't you remember any of the details, Sarah?"

"I'm afraid I can't. I've got something more important to do than to spend my time worrying about silly people who get themselves murdered in public places like the British Museum Reading Room."

"Was the other man murdered?" Henry could not restrain himself from asking these questions, though, knowing his sister as well as he did, he was perfectly aware that he could not really expect any satisfactory answers.

"How should I know?" she retorted. "As far as I remember, he died of heart failure, but quite possibly that was just the story that the papers told. Quite likely he was murdered, really, only they hushed it up. Maybe he was a relative of the Prime Minister, or the Chancellor of the Exchequer, or something, and they wanted to save money on death duties." Miss Fairhurst's ideas of the law and its complications were completely chaotic, and Henry, very wisely, did not attempt to argue with her on this score. He was intent on information, and thought that he should be able to get what he wanted from somewhere.

"I shall ring up Macgregor," he announced. "Maybe he will be able to find the information for me before he comes home tonight."

"That, I presume," said Sarah, very much on her dignity, "means that there will be a third to dinner tonight, and I, my dear Henry, shall have the unpleasant duty of persuading cook that she can make a joint purchased for two go around for three."

"And I'm sure," said Henry, now desiring to smooth her down, "that you will do the duty very successfully, my dear Sarah. No one can handle difficult servants more effectively than you can."

Angus Macgregor was a reporter on the *Post-Chronicle,* and as soon as dinner was over that night he produced a bulky bundle of press-cuttings from his pocket. He had long been a friend of Henry, and he often helped him with information culled from the organ of the Press for which he worked.

"Heaven knows what ye want this for, Henry, old man," he said. "Seems a bit out of your usual line to me. Still, you know your own business best, and I've got the information you asked for."

"You heard what I wanted, did you?" asked Henry. "We had a dreadful line, and I could scarcely hear what you were saying over the 'phone."

"Oh, yes, I heard all right," returned the other. "You wanted to know all about a man who died in the British Museum Reading Room about a year ago, or less. Reports of his death, details of the findings at the inquest, and so on. Though, as I said, why on earth ye wanted all this information is more than I can imagine."

"You'll know in good time, Macgregor," Henry told him. "In fact, I shouldn't be at all surprised if I could put you in the way of what I believe you call a scoop."

"What do you want to know first?" asked Macgregor.

"Who was the man?"

"His name was Wilkinson. He was Professor of English Literature at Northfield University."

"What?" Henry nearly jumped out of his skin. "Was he the great authority on the Elizabethan drama?"

"That's the fellow. Had some patent theory of his own that Shakespeare's plays were written by two people together— one was Shakespeare himself and the other Kit Marlowe. He worked it out very well, though 'twas all balderdash, of course."

"When did he die?"

"Let's see." Macgregor referred to the bundle of cuttings. "It's now June 20. It was exactly five months ago—on January 20 of this year."

"What was the verdict of the inquest?"

"Natural death. It was proved that he'd been suffering from some form of heart trouble—I don't understand the queer jargon of these doctor fellows. Still, everybody agreed that he was in such a condition that he might be expected to pop off at any moment, and it was just chance that he did so in the British Museum. He was handling some damned great book weighing about half a hundredweight, and he just collapsed on the floor and died. He was absolutely stone-dead before they could get him to the ambulance, let alone getting him near the hospital."

"Was there a post-mortem examination?" Again Macgregor consulted the papers he had brought with him from the office.

"It doesn't mention it here, and I shouldn't think that there was anything of the sort, or they'd have made a special point of reporting it," he said at length.

"Very careless of the coroner," said Henry.

Macgregor looked at him cautiously. "Why would ye say that, now?" he ventured to ask. "After all, the whole business, though it was a nasty business, taken all round, was not mysterious. 'Twas a clear enough case. The poor old devil had had a groggy heart for years, and 'twas just unlucky chance that it gave out in that gloomy old mausoleum, and not in some more pleasant place. Anyhow, I dare say that he would have been quite pleased at dying in such circumstances. He seems to have been a regular old bookworm, and to die among his books would please him."

"Difficult to explain, Macgregor, until I know a little more of the facts," said Henry.

"Well, what facts do ye want? I've got 'em all here—all that were made public, anyhow."

Henry sighed wearily. "Now, don't you start that stuff about things being concealed from the public," he warned his friend. "I get enough and to spare of that from Sarah, who thinks that there is a sort of conspiracy between the Press and the Government to keep all kinds of valuable information secret from her."

Macgregor grinned. "Ask your questions," he said. "If you think there's some fishy business going on here, and can give me the low-down on it, I can promise you that it'll be published from Land's End to John O' Groat's—and farther."

"At the moment," explained Henry, "that's the very thing that I don't want. After all, publication often ruins everybody's chances of catching a murderer."

Macgregor whistled. "So you think the dear old Professor of English Literature was murdered, do ye?" he asked. "And why would that idea be entering your sweet head, I wonder? After all, ye're not a suspicious man by nature, and don't look on all your fellow-men as sunk deep in iniquity, as every born journalist like myself does."

"Let me explain," said Henry. "Wilkinson was a Professor of English Literature in an English university."

Macgregor nodded. "Sceptic though I am," he said cheerfully, "I'll grant ye that."

"Curse that perverted sense of humour of yours," said Henry with a giggle. "Do please stop fooling in that way, and just listen to what I have to say."

"I'm all attention, me dear fellow," said Macgregor.

"He died," Henry went on, "apparently of heart-failure in the Reading Room of the British Museum some six months ago."

"Five," Macgregor interrupted.

"The dates are immaterial," said Henry. "He died in that way."

"Yes."

"Who gave evidence at the inquest?"

Once more Macgregor looked at the pile of papers that lay before him.

"His doctor, his son, and his friend," he announced at length.

"His friend?" Henry at once seized on what he thought was the important piece of information.

"Yes." Macgregor peered at the cutting. "Be damned," he said at length, "if I'm not the world's clumsiest fool. I've cut this paper so badly that a name is missing."

"What name?"

"The name of the friend."

"Can you get any of it? Any letters of it, I mean, so that there's some chance of seeing who the fellow is?"

"'Tis difficult," said Macgregor, peering into the smudgy print that lay before him. "It looks as if the name ends in two L's, though even there I can't be certain. You see, it comes at the top of a column, and with my clumsy scissors I've managed to slice off a piece of the damned paper, so that I can only make out the bottoms of the letters. And it may be they're some other letters."

Suddenly a thought came to Henry. It was a thought that almost made the meek little man's blood run cold, so amazing was it in its clarity.

"Does it say anything about what the friend did?" he asked. "After all, the friend of a Professor of English Literature might easily occupy some sort of official position in the university. It would be perfectly easy to trace him then, if he's a lecturer or anything."

"Good idea," said Macgregor. "Let's see. Oh, yes; Professor Emeritus in English Literature in Portavon University."

"God!" Henry's eyes nearly popped out of their sockets. He removed his pince-nez and polished them in an agitated manner.

"What's the matter with ye, man?" demanded Macgregor. "You're as white as a sheet. You look as if you're going to faint. Explain yourself, quick! Shall I get a drop of brandy? What the devil's the matter with you?"

Henry smiled the faintest of smiles. Then he perched his pince-nez perilously on his nose. He looked around him with what was almost a satisfied smile, and the colour slowly flowed back into his cheeks.

"Wull ye answer my questions, me mannie?" asked Macgregor, lapsing into his native dialect more and more in his agitation. "What the de'il's the matter wi' ye, that ye got so excited at that news? What the hell does it matter if the felly what gave evidence was professor at some crack-pot university in the south of England? Tell me."

"Only this," said Henry, and his voice was thin and clear. "Professor Julius Arnell, Professor Emeritus in the University of Portavon, died in the British Museum Reading Room this afternoon—died under my very eyes."

And Macgregor, old hand as he was at the tackling of mysterious crimes, felt his blood run cold within his veins.

Chapter IV

Miss Violet Arnell

"Now, Cunningham," said Shelley, with a smile. "What's the next move? Any suggestions?"

Cunningham ponderously considered the matter, frowning deeply.

"I should think, sir," he said, "that an interview with the old man's daughter would be the best thing."

"Capital idea," Shelley announced. "It's now—let me see—seven o'clock. Wonder if they're on the 'phone." He picked up a directory, ran his fingers rapidly down the columns, and found the number.

"Better ring her up," he added, "and more or less prepare her for the shock. After all, she's an only daughter, according to the reference books, and this will be a bit of a blow for her, I should think."

He asked for the number, and was soon in communication with Miss Violet Arnell.

"I'm afraid I have some bad news for you, Miss Arnell," Cunningham heard him say, when the preliminaries of identification had been got over.

"Yes," he went on. "Your father. He has met with a serious accident, and I shall have to come around and get some particulars about his work, and so forth. Will you be in for the evening? You will? Good. I will be around in three-quarters of an hour or less."

It was actually only about half an hour before they were driving along the main street of Pinner—a forlorn relic of the past, the village street of old-world charm, now surrounded by a wilderness of typically suburban red-brick and stucco, hideous in its unutilitarian sham-Gothic.

Professor Arnell had lived in a delightful old cottage, however, tucked away in a little side street off this main thoroughfare. It boasted a pleasant little flower garden and a fresh green lawn, and Shelley and Cunningham breathed in the fragrant scent of the stocks before they went to the front door.

Miss Violet Arnell was a kindly looking woman in the early thirties, her face and figure a modified and feminised version of her father's aggressiveness. What in him had become flaming red hair was in her a delightful shade of auburn. She was tall, lithe, and upright, and she greeted her visitors with a quiet smile, not unmingled with the sadness appropriate to the occasion.

There was no heart-broken grief or zealous anxiety in her voice, however, as she asked Shelley and Cunningham if they would each like to have a glass of sherry.

"Thank you, Miss Arnell," said Shelley; "I think I will. And I know that the Sergeant here never refuses a kindly offer of that sort."

Cunningham grinned somewhat sheepishly, and accepted the glass of excellent sherry which was placed in his hand.

"Now," she said, when these preliminaries were over, "what is all this about, Mr. Shelley? What has my father been up to? He's caused me plenty of worry with his absent-mindedness and his funny ways."

"You are quite prepared for a shock, then, Miss Arnell?" Shelley asked.

She nodded calmly. "Quite prepared for anything where my father is concerned," she replied.

"Your father," said Shelley bluntly, seeing that this girl was possessed of strong nerves, not likely to relapse into hysteria, "is dead."

Again she nodded, almost phlegmatically. "I feared as much when you warned me to be prepared for a shock," she said in quiet, unemotional tones.

"You are not surprised?"

"Why should I be?"

"Well, your father was by no means an old man. He was, I should think, almost in the prime of life. One does not feel surprise when a man of eighty years dies, but a man of your father's age…"

She interrupted swiftly. "My father has been in bad health for years," she said. "That was why he gave up his job at Portavon. He could not stand the strain of working regular hours. His heart was in a very groggy state, and there were days when he would stay in bed, just lying still and not daring to move, for fear the awful pain would come on again. Where did he die?"

"I think that this will probably be a worse shock than the news that he is dead," said Shelley. "He died in the Reading Room of the British Museum, and he was murdered."

Miss Arnell went white as a ghost. All the blood seemed to drain from her face, and she gripped the arms of the chair in which she sat. The veins on the back of her hands stood out in vivid relief against the sudden whiteness of her skin.

"Murdered? That can't be. Harry would never…" Her murmuring voice died away into sudden silence.

Swiftly Shelley seized on the point. "Harry would never do what?" he asked.

"Did I say Harry?" she asked in return, getting control of herself with obvious difficulty. "I don't know what I was talking about, Mr. Shelley. Honestly I think that the sudden shock must have sent my mind wandering along some strange bypaths of thought." The obvious artificiality of the phrase set Shelley pondering. What on earth, he asked himself, was the girl thinking of? There must be some reasonable explanation of this sudden change of face. Who was Harry? That was the obvious line of investigation.

"Had your father any friends who could give us information about him?" he asked, dissembling his interest in the hope that, if he could set her talking again, she might give herself away somehow.

"Not many," she said. "My father was rather a strange person. He made friends with great difficulty. I think that Professor Wilkinson of Northfield University and Dr. Crocker of Oxford were the only people who were really in his confidence over things—and they were really more acquaintances than friends, interested in the same subjects."

"I see," said Shelley thoughtfully. "And did they often visit him here?"

"Never." She was very emphatic. "No one ever came here except friends of mine."

"Friends of yours?" Here was his chance, Shelley thought, and grasped the opportunity without delay. "Could you mention any friends of yours who were in any way regular visitors to this house, Miss Arnell? You see, in a case like this it is important to get hold of anyone who knew your father, as we may be able to get some sort of pointer on his ways of thought—and a comparative stranger often notices more than an intimate relative like yourself."

There was a distinct pause before she replied. Then she said, slowly: "Miss Elizabeth Atkins. She's my closest friend. She was often here. But she didn't see much of father, I'm afraid. You see, he was the sort of man who keeps himself very much to himself, and he usually appeared only at meal-times if a visitor was here."

"What would he do at other times—other times than meal-times, I mean?"

"Just shut himself up in his study. He was a curious person, really, and I often thought it queer that a man like that should have a daughter like myself, fond of brightness and company." She showed every sign of going on with this line of thought, but Shelley was determined not to be led from the point, as he thought the conversation was just becoming of interest.

"Any other visitors?" he asked sharply.

"Well…" She appeared unwilling to answer this, and paused with an air of irresolution.

"Any men, for instance?" Shelley was intent on getting the information he required. "A man will often see something about other men which a woman will miss."

"There is Mr. Baker," she conceded.

"Who is he?"

"He is the teacher of science at the school around the corner here."

Shelley smiled gently. "And does he come here very often?" he asked.

"Very often," she replied, and paused again. "You see… you see…I am going to marry him."

"And did your father approve of the engagement?"

Miss Arnell paused for a moment, and then burst into tears. Her whole body shook with great sobs. She was convulsed with sorrow, and wept as if her heart would break.

"I think," she managed to blurt out between great bursts of tears, "that you are most unfair. The way that you worm things out of people. It may be your idea of doing a gentleman's job in life, Mr. Shelley, but it's not mine."

Shelley looked at her sternly. "You seem to forget, Miss Arnell," he said, "that your father was murdered. My job is not to deal with things in any kid-glove fashion, but to obtain all the information which seems to me at all likely to help in the investigation. I have no desire to hurt anyone, but one must occasionally be brutal in order to find out what is necessary in solving a very difficult problem."

She dried her eyes on a microscopic handkerchief. "I understand, Mr. Shelley," she said, gulping back her sobs. "If you want to ask any more questions I shall be pleased to answer them as well as I can."

"I presume," said Shelley, without further comment, "that your father did *not* approve of your engagement to Mr. Harry Baker." The "Harry" was a shot in the dark, and Shelley was pleased to observe that she apparently did not notice the assumption.

"No," she said. "He thought that Harry was just a fortune-hunter, after my money, and that I should get someone much better and richer for a husband."

"I suppose," said Shelley, "that there is a good deal of money in your family."

"Oh yes," she replied more cheerfully. "Father was a very rich man, you know. I don't know where his money will be left, but there must be a will somewhere."

"Who are his lawyers?"

"Samuel, Grant, and Samuel, of Chancery Lane."

"Make a note of that, Cunningham," said Shelley. "We shall have to see them tomorrow."

"And anything else?" she asked.

"Your fiancé's name and address."

"Henry Baker, Manor School."

"That's close to here, I think you said."

"Yes. In the next street."

"Well," Shelley went on, "I think that is about all for the moment, Miss Arnell. Oh, there is one thing more. Do you happen to know if your father was fond of almonds? The sugar-coated ones, I mean."

She smiled. "His one vice, I called it," she said. "He would chew sugared almonds all day long. He was not a heavy smoker, and he drank very little, so he used to say that he was entitled to his one little bit of dissipation."

"Did he always buy them at one particular shop? A man with the habit of eating some particular kind of sweetmeat often does, you know," Shelley explained.

"Yes, he did. He always bought them from a shop in the High Street here—a Mr. Martin sold them. I think they were some special brand that weren't obtainable elsewhere. Father always said that he couldn't get almonds from anywhere else that tasted half as nice."

"Mr. Martin, High Street," murmured Cunningham, writing the address down in his notebook.

"Did every one know that your father had this little peculiarity—this fancy for sugared almonds?" asked Shelley.

"He didn't make any secret of it, if that's what you mean," she replied. "I should imagine that anyone who knew him at all well would be aware of it."

"Anyone such as Dr. Wilkinson, for instance, or Mr. Baker," Shelley suggested.

"Why, yes…But I don't understand. Why all this interest in father's taste in sweets?" She looked puzzled at the trend of the conversation.

Shelley thought that this was another occasion when brutal frankness was indicated. A little shock might make her give away further facts. And that she was hiding things which were better revealed he felt very certain. So he said: "Because those sugared almonds brought your father to his death, Miss Arnell. He was poisoned by an almond containing potassium cyanide." This was mere guesswork, but Shelley thought he was quite safe in anticipating the findings of the medical men.

"Poisoned. How dreadful!" In despite of the words, however, she did not seem more shocked than she had been before. Her tongue seemed now to be uttering the correct sentiments unconsciously, while her mind was far away.

"Yes, poisoned, Miss Arnell," said Shelley. "And my job—unpleasant though it may be—is to find out who poisoned him. That's a job that you may be sure I shall carry out to the end, no matter where it may lead."

Precisely how this conversation might have proceeded it would be difficult to say, for at this moment the telephone bell rang, and, with a brief "Excuse me," Violet Arnell lifted the receiver.

"Hullo," she said. "Yes. Who is that, please? Yes; I will tell him."

She turned to Shelley, and held the receiver towards him. "It's for you, Mr. Shelley," she explained. "A message from Scotland Yard."

"Thanks," he said briefly, and spoke into the receiver. "Shelley speaking," he snapped. "What is it? Who?" Then he paused for a moment, obviously listening to a long piece of conversation from the other end. Cunningham strained his ears, but was unable to understand a word, being able only to hear a subdued buzz.

"Yes," said Shelley again. "Fairhurst. Yes. What? The devil he has? Who? Wilkinson? Right. I'll be back right away."

Cunningham and Miss Arnell sat in silence while Shelley banged down the receiver, and turned towards them, an air of almost desperate eagerness about him.

"Important information has just come through from the Yard, Miss Arnell," he said. "I shall have to get back to London right away. I hope that if I want any more information from you I shall be able to get hold of you at any time. Shall I? Good. Then come along, Cunningham. We've no time to waste. Must get on without delay."

In the High Street again, Shelley grasped Cunningham's arm tightly. "Listen," he said. "Wilkinson is dead. Fairhurst found it out."

"Fairhurst?" Cunningham was amazed. "That little worm couldn't be a murderer, surely."

"He's been dead for months, apparently," said Shelley. "I couldn't get much sense out of them, though. I must get back to the Yard to sift this information, and I want you to get hold of this man Baker. Grill him all you can, and see if he has any sort of alibi for yesterday. That's not vitally important, as anyone might have put the poisoned sweet in Arnell's packet at any time, knowing that he'd be certain to eat it sooner or later. Still, it's a point worth investigating. Hope to God he isn't on the 'phone. Still, you must try to get him before the fair Violet has had time to warn him."

"Any particular points, chief?" asked Cunningham eagerly. This was a great rise for him, to be given the job of questioning the man who was at any rate temporarily the principal suspect.

"No. I leave that to your discretion entirely. You know my methods, Watson," said Shelley with a grin. "I must get back to the Yard. I must hie me to London."

"And I must hie me to Baker," said Cunningham. "Wonder what he'll have to say."

"Not much," said Shelley. But he was wrong.

Chapter V

Cunningham Investigates

It was with some trepidation that Cunningham approached the entrance to the school. It was a boarding-school, and some of the staff, including Mr. Henry Baker, "lived in." Cunningham felt both elated and worried, for this was the first occasion on which he had undertaken such an onerous task. However, as soon as the bright maid who answered the door had seen him comfortably seated in the neat little sitting-room, and had promised to go in search of Mr. Baker, he felt his wonted air of quiet confidence returning to him, and planned out in his mind the way in which he proposed to tackle this important witness.

Soon Mr. Baker came in. He was a man of medium height, his hair was dark, his eyes, if a trifle too close-set, were of a pleasant brown colour, and in their depths a sense of humour sparkled and twinkled.

"Well, Sergeant," he said jovially as he approached, his hand held out in candid friendship; "what's the trouble, eh? What am I to be run in for this time?"

"Nothing, I hope, sir," replied Cunningham, smiling in his turn. "It is only that I want some information from you.

We understand that you know something about a case which we have under investigation." Cunningham did not often play the "heavy detective," but he felt that the present was one of the few occasions when such a rôle would be suitable.

"Right ho!" responded Baker. "Fire away! Can't think what crook I can number among my acquaintances, but I dare say that you know more about the criminal classes than I do."

"It's in connection with the death of Professor Arnell," Cunningham began, and paused. Baker looked at him with an air of absolute astonishment that seemed too genuine to be "faked." This man, Cunningham told himself, couldn't possibly be the murderer. Or, if he was, he must also be a consummate actor in order to assume this appearance of complete surprise, not unmixed with consternation.

"Did I hear you say the *death* of Professor Arnell?" asked Baker.

Cunningham nodded. "Yes," he said bluntly. "Professor Arnell died in London today."

"Poor old chap!" exclaimed Baker. "Of course, I know that he's had a groggy heart for years. Still, this will be a hell of a shock for Violet." Then he paused suddenly, as if a new idea had suddenly come into his head. "But—I say, Sergeant," he asked. "What are you doing here? I mean to say, there's nothing fishy, nothing suspicious about the old man's death, is there?"

"Only too suspicious, I'm afraid, sir," answered Cunningham with a gloomy nod.

"You don't say! Too bad! Poor old Violet will feel it terribly that her father has committed suicide."

"Did I mention suicide, sir?" Cunningham asked quietly.

"No, now I come to think of it, you didn't. But...but... you can't mean," asked Baker, his eyes opening widely, "you can't mean—*murder?*"

"I'm afraid, sir," Cunningham explained, "that we have only too sure grounds for suspecting that the professor was murdered. He died in the British Museum Reading Room. We have every reason for thinking that he was poisoned with a dose of cyanide."

"Good God!" If Baker had been surprised before he was doubly astonished now. His face had gone white as a sheet, and now the blood was slowly flowing back into his countenance. Cunningham thought that this was too genuine to be assumed. Although, of course, he told himself, it was possible that the man had committed the murder, and had imagined that he was going to get away with it. It was possible that the sudden realisation that the police were on his track was sufficient shock to bring about this air of astonishment and horror. Anyhow, Cunningham had thought out his plan of campaign, and he was determined to follow it to the bitter end.

"I shall have to ask you a few questions, sir, as you will, of course, realise," he said.

"Of course," said Baker; "though what the devil you expect me to tell you about him I'm damned if I know. I wasn't exactly a bosom pal of his, as I expect you've found out already."

"We know that you were engaged to his daughter, sir," Cunningham explained.

"And I expect you've also discovered that he didn't precisely weep on the shoulder of his prospective son-in-law," added Baker, with a somewhat sheepish grin.

"Yes; we've discovered that."

"What else do you wish to discover? If there's anything I can tell you I'll do so like a shot—although I don't for a moment expect that there is."

"Well, we can but try, sir. First of all, merely as a matter of routine, can you give me an account of your own movements today? You understand, I expect, that this is the sort of question that we have to put to every one who is at all likely to be connected with the case—and, after all, some evil-minded people might be inclined to suggest, if you had no alibi, that you had a motive for getting rid of the professor." Cunningham gave himself a mental pat on the back. He thought that he had managed that in quite diplomatic fashion.

Baker chuckled. "And you yourself would be the first of those evil-minded people, I think, Mr. Cunningham," he said. "Right. My movements today. Nine-thirty to twelve-thirty, teaching a group of foolish youngsters the rudiments of chemistry—rudiments which they have no doubt forgotten again long before this moment. Twelve-thirty to two, lunching in the company of said boys. Two-thirty to four-thirty, umpiring a cricket match on the school playing-field. Four-thirty, having tea until five-thirty. May seem a long time, but we lingered over cigarettes afterwards. Five-thirty to seven, correcting rottenly written exercise-books. Seven to the moment of your arrival, having dinner and then playing billiards with one of my companions in iniquity, the mathematics master. How's that, Sergeant?"

"A hundred not out, I should think, sir," said Cunningham, not showing by a single movement of a muscle that this neat recital of times had impressed him not a whit. He was remembering Shelley's remark that really this matter of alibis was of no vital importance, it being likely that the poisoned sweet had been placed in the packet at some earlier date, the murderer being sure that the Professor would eat it sooner or later.

"Good. And the next question, please." Cunningham did not altogether like the flippant way in which this young man was treating the murder of his prospective father-in-law, but he realised that he must not allow a dislike of the young man's manner to make him in any way suspicious of

Baker. Outward appearance, Shelley had often said, was the one thing which the good detective had perforce to school himself to distrust.

"Another routine one, I think, sir," he said briskly. "Can you suggest anyone who would wish to kill the professor? Had he, in other words, any enemy or enemies who would wish him out of the way?"

Baker thought. "The law of libel or slander or whatever the legal lingo is may be disregarded on this privileged occasion, I take it?" he said.

"Yes," said Cunningham with a grin. "If you have any suspicions, though they're only vague, I should advise you to bring them out into the daylight."

"Number one," said Baker; "if I were in your shoes I should interview a young man called Moses Moss. He is, as his name should indicate, a Jew. He is also a nephew of Professor Arnell. He is also, if I am not mistaken, Professor Arnell's principal heir."

"Why," exclaimed Cunningham in surprise, "won't the professor have left all his money to his daughter?"

"I think not," answered the young man. "You see, the professor was always threatening to cut her off with a farthing if she didn't give up her penniless suitor. And she was always asserting her right to marry whoever she damned well liked. I shouldn't be at all surprised if the professor, in a fit of temper, had left all his money to Mr. Moss. Mind you, I may be quite wrong. But I have my suspicions. Anyhow, that's a little hint."

"Where can I find this Mr. Moss, sir?" asked Cunningham, producing his note book for the first time during this interview.

"I don't quite know where he hangs out—somewhere in Bloomsbury, I fancy," answered Baker. "But you can find him any afternoon in Sally's Club, in St. Martin's Lane."

"Sally's Club, St. Martin's Lane," murmured Cunningham. "What sort of club is that, sir?" he asked. "Social, literary, what?"

"Just a place where one can drink when the pubs are shut," said Baker. "I've only been there once in my life. My screw doesn't run to gin—good old beer is about all that I can manage, and the beer there is awful stuff."

"I see," said Cunningham. "Sally's Club. Right. We will see Mr. Moss tomorrow. What sort of terms was he on with the professor?"

"Outwardly friendly," said Baker. "In fact, he was always 'sucking up,' as my boys would elegantly express it. But I have long had a suspicion that he was not so fond of the old man as he so often pretended. Personally, I think that he was just eagerly anticipating the future, if you follow me."

"Did he know that the professor had rather strong feelings about his daughter's fiancé?" asked Cunningham.

"Yes," answered Baker with a cheery grin. "Everyone who came into contact with the old man knew all about that. After all, when one feels something as strongly as he felt my ineligibility, one is apt to let the feeling come to the surface at any time."

"I see." Cunningham paused, and racked his brains for the next question, which he knew must be hiding its gentle head somewhere. "But," he added, suddenly remembering a previous remark, "I think you said that he was suspect number one, didn't you, sir?"

"I did," answered Baker rather grimly. "Suspect number two is Dr. Crocker, an old snob from Oxford."

"Why do you think he is a suspect, sir?"

"Because he hated Arnell like poison. Absolutely loathed the sight of him, and didn't make any attempt to hide the fact, either."

"What was the reason for this hate of his?"

"Just professional jealousy, I think." Baker smiled. "Some years ago Dr. Crocker produced some patent theory of his own about the authorship of Shakespeare's plays. You know, some cryptogram or cipher idea, like the Baconians produce so proudly. Something completely crazy, and yet logical in a silly sort of way, if you understand."

"I understand," said Cunningham, who had so far been fortunate enough not to meet with this particular brand of literary lunacy.

"Well," Baker went on, "Arnell read the book which the Oxford johnnie produced, and reviewed it for some learned journal or other. Previous to that they had been very good friends, but now he simply chewed up Crocker's theory, so that the man absolutely hadn't a leg to stand on. And Crocker wrote nasty letters to all the literary papers—letters which they usually refused to publish—pointing out what an utter old fool Arnell was. After that little episode, of course, their friendship just faded away and died."

"When did this happen, sir?" asked Cunningham. "Have you got any idea of the dates?"

"It would be some time last summer, I should think," was the reply. "July or August, or thereabouts. At any rate, if you say about twelve months ago, you wouldn't be far out."

"And did this enmity go on, sir?"

"Oh, yes. In fact, it showed every sign of getting worse. And Arnell was working on a book of Shakespearian criticism, in which he proposed, I believe, to destroy every Shakespearian critic of past and present, from Sir Edward Durning-Lawrence and J. M. Robertson, down to G. B. Harrison and Dr. Crocker. Not that Crocker was really a Shakespearian critic. Marlowe and Greene and all those lesser Elizabethans were really his province, just as they were Arnell's."

"But I understood from Miss Arnell that Dr. Crocker was a friend of the professor," Cunningham objected.

"Oh, did she say that?" Baker smiled once more. "Arnell was one of the real old-fashioned brigade where women were concerned. I expect that accounts for her not knowing about this quarrel. He held that a woman's job was in the home, looking after man's worldly needs, and taking care of the children, if the good God saw fit to give her any. He always said that a man's job was his own affair, and that a woman shouldn't expect to share his interests. So I suppose, although he talked to me endlessly about the iniquities of the scholar from Oxford, that he never bothered to mention the subject to her at all."

"H'm." Cunningham didn't think that this sounded at all convincing, though he was well aware that, even in this modern world of ours, there were still people who held such old-fashioned views.

"Did Professor Arnell ever correspond with Dr. Crocker?" he asked.

"In the past quite a lot," answered Baker. "Not since the quarrel, however. I remember he had a letter from Crocker saying that in view of his discourteous and unscholarly conduct he could consider their friendship at an end. He spoke of getting the letter framed, as a proof that he was one critic who did not spend half his time boosting his friends' books, like so many of them seem to do."

"I see." Cunningham paused again. "Well, sir, does that exhaust your suspicions?"

"I think so," said Baker slowly. "Unless I suspect Violet and myself, as I'm sure you must be doing inside that discreet mind of yours, Sergeant."

Laughingly Cunningham disclaimed such unworthy suspicions, though he feared that his denial must sound strangely unconvincing to the other man. After all, Baker was the obvious person to be suspected. And he was a science master in a school, which meant that he would be able to get hold of some cyanide if he wanted it.

"Anyhow," Baker added, as he accompanied the detective to the door, "you can be assured that I shan't run away, Sergeant. I shall be on duty here until the end of term, which is—alas!—two or three weeks away yet. And I hope that you'll have the guilty person under lock and key long before then, Sergeant, don't you?"

"I hope so too, sir," said Cunningham, but there was little conviction in his tone.

It was not until he was waiting on the platform of the railway station that Cunningham felt himself at leisure to consider what his information really amounted to, to sum up in a few sentences what he had learned, and to decide precisely how he would tell Shelley what he had discovered.

Baker had a complete alibi for the day. That was the first point. Moses Moss was the next suspect, and Dr. Crocker, to whom they had already had the attention drawn, would follow. The question of the will of Professor Arnell, Shelley already had under consideration, and no doubt they would have got hold of most of the other points without Baker's assistance, willingly though it had been given.

Then Cunningham smacked his knee so hard and so resoundingly that an old lady sitting opposite him looked up in alarm.

"What a fool!" he said to himself. "Why on earth didn't I think of that before?" He had forgotten to test Baker on the question of his last contact with the professor, the occasion when, if at all, he would have placed the poisoned sweet in the packet!

Chapter VI

New Information

Mr. Henry Fairhurst twisted himself uncomfortably in the deep leather-padded chair. The policeman at the other side of the room cast suspicious glances at the little man, as if he thought that the pince-nez hid eyes of implacable evil. Mr. Fairhurst twisted again. If this was the way Scotland Yard treated a man bringing valuable information, he told himself, he would not come near the place again. He might have been the suspect in a murder trial, for all the deference with which they dealt with him. And yet he had brought them the most important discovery which had been made in connection with the murder.

They had kept him waiting for hours, too. Since he first told his story to a grim-visaged detective he had been planted in this arm-chair, a suspicious policeman on the other side of the room, and had been bluntly requested to await further developments, to sit tight until some other unspecified individual turned up. On this mysterious gentleman's arrival, Mr. Fairhurst had been led to suspect that he would have to tell his tale again.

Soon his unfortunate dilemma was cleared up, however, for Inspector Shelley burst into the room, rubbing his hands briskly together, and with a twinkle of pleasure in his keen grey eyes.

"Sorry to have kept you waiting so long, Mr. Fairhurst," he said smilingly, "but the fact of the matter is that I have been out of London since you saw me last—interviewing important witnesses in this case."

"That's quite all right, Inspector," Henry returned, "and I can assure you that I didn't mind waiting." (Politeness makes liars of us all!)

Shelley looked at the little man keenly. "I understand, Mr. Fairhurst," he remarked, "that you have some sort of new information for us."

Henry drew himself up to his full five feet four inches, replying with an air of great dignity: "Indeed I have, Inspector. Some most surprising new information at that. Something, if I am not mistaken, which will make you sit up and open your eyes in astonishment."

"Takes a good deal to astonish Scotland Yard, sir," was the reply to this. "Still, you may be right. I understand that you want to tell us something about the death of Professor Wilkinson of Northfield University."

Henry Fairhurst nodded emphatically. "When I got home, Inspector, after I had given you what information I could about the death of Professor Arnell, I began, as you might well imagine, to think over all the details of the case."

"Quite so," said Shelley non-committally.

"And then it occurred to me that I had read somewhere that another man recently died in the Reading Room at the British Museum." Henry thought that there was no especial point in speaking of his sister's remembrance of this other death. After all, if there was any credit going in this matter, he might as well get it, and Sarah would really never be aware of what she had missed.

"Really?" Shelley's eyebrows rose interrogatively. He in his turn was prepared to do some bluffing. The little man would be much more likely to give out all the information which was at his disposal if he was encouraged to think that his facts were not in any way astonishing, but was permitted to imagine that he could merely confirm information already received from other sources. Shelley may have looked simple enough, but in actuality he was far from it, as many an over-confident criminal had found to his cost.

"Yes," said Henry. "And I got into touch with a friend who works on one of the London daily papers, and enquired if he remembered anything about such a case."

"And did he?" Shelley was unable to restrain his eagerness now, as he began to realise whither this conversation was leading.

"He did. He remembered that the man who had died in the Reading Room of the British Museum some six months ago was Professor Wilkinson of Northfield University." Henry was satisfied that his new information was of the most sensational kind, and he was frankly disappointed at the matter-of-fact way in which the Scotland Yard man took it.

"But why do you think that such a death, taking place some six months ago, necessarily had anything to do with the present murder?" asked Shelley.

"Well…" This point had apparently not occurred to Henry. "But it is surely obvious…" he said, and paused irresolutely.

"What is obvious, Mr. Fairhurst?"

"Surely if two men, each experts in one particular branch of knowledge, each die in one spot, even though their deaths are separated by some months, there is some presumption that their deaths are in some way connected."

"A possibility, but by no means a presumption," Shelley corrected him. "After all, there have been remarkable coincidences of that sort before, and no doubt there will be again. It is by no means impossible that this is a coincidence."

"Do you really think so?"

"I don't think anything about it yet. I want to know all the facts of the man's death. Do you know anything about it? What verdict did the coroner's jury bring in—for I assume that there was an inquest, since it was apparently a sudden death? What was the medical evidence? Was there any indication that Professor Wilkinson, like our friend Arnell, was poisoned? You see, Mr. Fairhurst, there are all sorts of questions to be settled before we come to any kind of conclusion as to whether the two deaths are connected by anything more than mere coincidence." Shelley was quite breathless after this tirade, but he was pleased to observe, by the look of bewilderment that had gradually spread over Fairhurst's face, that he was producing the desired impression. He felt sure that Fairhurst would be a useful witness; but not if he persisted in twisting every fact to fit some pet theory of his own.

"It was proved that he was suffering from some sort of heart trouble," said Fairhurst. "Everybody seemed to know that—but then, for all I know, Arnell may also have had a weak heart."

Shelley nodded. "He had," he said briefly.

"He was apparently handling a heavy book of some sort, and he just collapsed and died. They brought in a verdict of death from natural causes."

"And that," said Shelley, "was that."

"As far," added Henry cautiously, "as we know at the present moment."

"Yes," said Shelley, and held out his hand to the little man. "Thank you very much for your information, Mr. Fairhurst, which I hope will be of some use to us. I will notify you when the inquest takes place, and what you will probably be asked there."

"But, my dear Inspector," protested Henry, "am I to know no more about this? I...I have given you some most important information, I...I have given you a hint which may be the point deciding the whole case. Am I to know nothing about what is done in the way of acting on this information?"

Shelley smiled. "The papers, my dear Mr. Fairhurst," he said, "have a habit of reporting criminal cases in some fullness. And if your information is really important I might even be able to get you a seat at the Old Bailey for the trial."

"But until then," Henry began.

"Until then," Shelley continued, "I fear that we cannot disclose any of our information, even to you, my dear Mr. Fairhurst."

And with that Henry Fairhurst had perforce to be content.

He would, however, have been pleased if he could have seen the flurry of activity into which his story plunged Scotland Yard immediately after his departure.

Shelley rang bells and spoke into telephones. He visited various departments and talked to many people. Finally he sent for a certain gentleman at Scotland Yard who is known as the memory of the Yard, for his was an encyclopædic knowledge of all mysterious characters, all criminal cases, all sudden deaths within recent years. He was, in fact, a walking dictionary of crime.

"Look here, Mac," said Shelley, when he arrived, "can you remember anything about the death of a fellow called Professor Wilkinson of Northfield University—happened six months or so back?"

Mac thought for a minute or so. "I'll no say that I can remember all about yon fella," he admitted, "but I can tell ye a bit aboot him."

"Good," said Shelley. "Carry on."

"Died in Reading Room of British Museum," said Mac, speaking in a sharp, jerky manner, almost as if reading a series of notes from a page. "Age 55. Height…"

"Don't bother about measurements and so on," said Shelley. "I can look them up at leisure. I want the facts about his death, verdict at the inquest, medical details, and all that sort of thing."

"Verdict, natural causes," went on Mac, unperturbed. "He was supposed to have had some sort o' heart failure, but there was, if I remember aright, some doot aboot the question."

"Why," asked Shelley, "what was the doubt?"

"Och, 'twas nothin'," answered Mac. "'Twas only that he left a good deal o' cash to a young schoolmaister in the country somewhere, and the young fella was in the Readin' Room on the same day as the old chap died. And when that sort o' thing happens, ye ken, there are aye folks unco' ready to put twa and twa thegither, and mak' 'em five."

Shelley looked up in surprise. This was suggestive of a new line of investigation. It was new information with a vengeance. He felt that he knew the answer to his next question before he asked it—yet he was impelled to ask it, just the same.

"What was the name of the young schoolmaster? Does it happen to stick in that queer old head of yours, Mac?" he asked, with a grin.

"It does," returned Mac, unabashed, for his phenomenal memory he regarded much as other people regard their hair or their teeth—as a fact of nature, to be accepted, but not necessarily to be in any way proud of. "The young fella's name was Henry Baker. He was Wilkinson's cousin."

Once again, as so many times before in his career, Shelley was up against an acute problem. Many impetuous men would, on receipt of this information, have hurried off to arrest the young man at once, but Shelley realised that it was quite possible, in spite of the undoubtedly serious evidence against him, that he was innocent. In any case, he was probably quite safely stowed away at Pinner—and Cunningham would have some more facts and theories about him to be added to the rapidly growing accumulation.

"Thank you, Mac," he said, not showing in his face the feeling of delight that was surging up within him. "That's very useful. I hope it'll lead to our getting our man once again."

"Don't thank me," said Mac. "'Tis nothing, I assure ye. Nothing more than a little gift, that the government underpays me for using." And he stalked out of the room, leaving Shelley with a smile still on his face, for Mac's perpetual grumbles at the smallness of his salary (which was actually not so small, after all) were one of the standing jokes among the higher ranks at Scotland Yard.

Shelley drew a sheet of paper towards him, and, as was his wont when in the middle of a difficult case, wrote out a summary of what he had as yet discovered. Several people would have been surprised if they could have read what he wrote, for Shelley, as has already been noted, could on occasions appear disarmingly simple when, in reality, he was laying traps of the deepest guile.

Then he took another sheet of paper, headed it "Immediate Jobs," and then chewed the end of his pen reflectively. What he afterwards wrote was this:

"(1) ? Exhume Wilkinson. See Home Secretary. ? Is cyanide traceable long after death.

"(2) Make sure of facts about Baker's presence in B.M. when Wilkinson died. ? Find if Baker has alibi on occasion of death of Arnell. P.S.—Alibi not worth much in any case, since poisoned sweet may have been placed in bag some time before.

"(3) See about Arnell's will—also Wilkinson's? Is any one beneficiary of both, save Baker, who benefits *via* Violet Arnell in second case, and directly in first case.

"(4) Does Dr. Crocker of Oxford know anything about these two? Can he help in suggesting motives, since he is apparently a friend of both of them?

"(5) Were there any personal quarrels in which the two men were concerned? Any enemy of the two, apart from mercenary motives."

He put down his pen and sighed deeply. "The questions seem to be endless," he murmured. "Suppose I'm trying to theorise too soon. Must wait until I've got more facts to work upon. At the moment things look pretty black for Mr. Baker, but then at this stage in the case it's impossible to go at all deeply into questions of motive, and so on. Where the devil is Cunningham?"

There was a bell on the desk before him, and he pressed it. A constable appeared. "Has Sergeant Cunningham returned yet?" asked Shelley.

"No, sir."

"Well, when he does, tell him to report to me at once. I shall stay here until his return, as he will have some important information on this case," Shelley snapped.

"Very well, sir."

The constable retired, and Shelley studied the document before him—the list of jobs to be immediately done, questions to be settled without delay.

What was there here which he could make up his mind to do straight away? He probably had some hours to waste before Cunningham returned, and he might as well employ those hours in a more or less profitable manner, he told himself.

Then he looked up in pleasant anticipation. Question number four. That could be decided without delay. Dr.

Crocker of Oxford might be at home. Anyhow, he could communicate with the Oxford police, and then, if the man was in residence (it was still vacation time, so he might be climbing the Alps, or doing whatever else Oxford dons did in their holidays), he would be able to run down to Oxford on the following morning, and find out what he had to say about his two dead friends.

Shelley drew the telephone towards him. "Get me Oxford police," he instructed the operator.

In a few minutes he was speaking to the inspector in charge of the City police station at Oxford, and he explained his need for information, having first given the secret police sign which indicates that a fellow limb of the law is making the enquiry.

"I want," he said, "to know something about a Dr. Crocker, who occupies some sort of official position in Oxford."

"Certainly," said the rich voice of the man at the other end—probably, Shelley decided, a fat man fond of his glass of beer. "Lecturer in English Literature at St. Francis's College here."

"What sort of fellow is he?" asked Shelley.

"Tall—six feet one—thin, grey hair, blue eyes," the other man began.

"I don't mean that. What sort of fellow is he in character? Reliable?"

"Straight as a die."

"Do you know him personally?" asked Shelley, thinking that if the man in Oxford knew the object of his investigations it might be possible, by discreet questioning, to get the required information without the trouble and time which a visit to Oxford would entail.

"No."

"Is he a well-known character in the city?"

"No."

"Well, how do you know so much about him?"

"Well, we've been hunting for him for a week."

"Hunting?" Shelley was absolutely astounded. What on earth, he asked himself, did this mean?

"Yes. You see, Doctor Crocker disappeared last Sunday, and hasn't been seen since!"

Chapter VII

The Fate of Dr. Crocker

"This is a perfectly crazy case, Cunningham," Shelley remarked. "It strikes me that someone with a lunatic idea about English literature is setting about eliminating all the great authorities on Elizabethan drama which the country possesses. Here's Arnell dead, and Wilkinson dead, and Crocker vanished—Heaven knows who will be the next one to do a disappearing trick."

Cunningham grinned uneasily. He never felt very happy when his chief became flippant. It boded ill for someone, but it often indicated that all was not going as well as might be hoped.

"Any trace of this man Crocker, sir?" he asked, and Shelley shook his head. It was an angry gesture, and showed that the events of the past few hours had not been particularly good for the inspector's nerves.

"No," he answered. "Why the hell we keep a squad of men here, with the special job of looking after missing people, I can't think. They don't know their job, Cunningham, that's what's the matter." Savagely he pressed a bell-push which was on his desk, and a sleepy-looking policeman appeared. His sleepiness annoyed Shelley even more, though the fact that it was now 1 a.m. should have been enough to account for the matter.

"Send Sergeant Owens to me at once," Shelley ordered.

"I don't know if he's gone home or not, sir," replied the constable.

Shelley grinned. But there was no humour in his grin, merely an angry satisfaction that his tangled mind was involving others. Cunningham was surprised. Not for years had he known the chief to be so worried and upset. This case, he told himself, had "got Shelley's goat," and got it with a vengeance!

He listened. Shelley was speaking. "He must be here," he said, with some satisfaction. "He has my orders not to go home until some information comes through—and if it had come through he would have brought it to me without delay."

"Very good, sir," said the constable, with the air of a sleepy butler, and retired.

Soon Sergeant Owens came in. He too was worried and upset. He realised that the disappearance of a noted Oxford don (and a don with a cousin in the Cabinet!) was something that simply cried out for investigation. And he was only too well aware that as yet his investigations had not brought in the results which those in authority would be certain, ere long, to demand.

"Now, Owens," said Shelley briskly, "how is the search going?"

"Not too well, I'm afraid, sir," answered Owens apologetically.

"Huh!" Shelley's exclamation was a wordless grunt, but it was far more expressive of his annoyance and disgust than a long and sarcastic sentence would have been.

"We've traced the hotel where he usually stays in London, sir," he said. "It's the Prince's, in Bayswater. He hasn't been there for three months or more."

"Go on."

"He has various friends in London. Mr. Lucas, the scientist, who lives at Hampstead, is one. He's not seen him, but he had a letter yesterday saying that Crocker would be in town within the next week or two, and would be calling. He said he'd drop him a line later, and let him know day and time and so on."

"That's a point that would be worth following up," Shelley remarked. "Did he give any reason for this visit to London?"

"None. But then that's nothing unusual, for Lucas was quite accustomed to receiving such letters from Crocker. He said that Crocker was often in town to do some work at the British Museum. He did a lot of reading and research there, and…"

Shelley interrupted him. "I've a 'hunch,' Owens," he said. "Cunningham!"

"Yes, sir," answered Cunningham, prompt as ever.

"Do you happen to know if there's anyone on duty at the British Museum now?"

"Sure to be some caretakers or something, I should think," said Cunningham.

"I didn't ask what you *think*," Shelley snapped. "I asked if you *knew*."

"No, sir."

"Well, ring up, and find out. If there's a caretaker, get him to let us in, and tell him to get the keys of the Reading Room if he can. We shall be around there in a few minutes, and then we shall see what we shall see."

The Reading Room was a strangely deserted place when they entered it. The caretaker had switched on the lights, but the tall, domed room, its shadows fading off into the mysterious darknesses of the roof, was curiously eerie and weird. Cunningham, hard-boiled materialist though he was, found himself shuddering and glancing behind him as if he feared that some unseen assassin was on his track.

But, in spite of Shelley's insistent "hunch," they found no trace of Dr. Crocker. There was not a soul in the room except themselves. They peered behind desks and under tables. Shelley even insisted on going up to the metal galleries which run around the room, but the place was deserted and still as the grave.

Shelley's temper, which had been bad enough before, was now in the vilest mood that Cunningham had ever seen it. The inspector was hungry, thirsty, tired, and sleepy. He had worked very hard for several hours, and he felt that he had nothing to show for it.

"Back to the Yard," he said shortly, and they made their way to the door, the caretaker locking the doors behind them, and escorting them down to the big iron gates which led to Great Russell Street.

As they approached the gates Shelley looked around him with sudden interest.

"What's that?" he asked.

"What's what?" asked Cunningham in his turn.

"That…over there," said Shelley, pointing.

Cunningham looked in the direction indicated, but could see nothing at all.

"Has it been raining at all today?" asked Shelley.

"Why, no," said Cunningham.

"Well, there's a pool of something on the concrete path over there," said Shelley. "I caught a flash as the light of the street lamp was reflected in it."

"Expect that they've been washing the path," Cunningham suggested, but Shelley laughed the idea to scorn.

"Do you really think so?" he asked. "Well, let's have a look at it. Have you got a torch with you?" Cunningham nodded. "Well, get it out, and then we can see."

They strode towards the spot that Shelley had indicated, and Cunningham produced his electric torch, shining it at his chief's directions. There was certainly a pool of liquid there. But the liquid was not water.

"What the devil?" Cunningham muttered.

"Not the devil," Shelley corrected him, with an eerie chuckle. "The murderer."

"What do you mean, sir?" Cunningham asked.

Shelley stooped and touched the little pool of liquid. It was unpleasantly sticky.

"Blood, Cunningham," he said. "There's been something very queer going on whilst we were inside that building."

Cunningham was flashing the light around him, trying to pierce the gloom and to see whether there was any sensible explanation of this strange affair.

"Look!" he suddenly exclaimed, and Shelley looked at the torch-beam, cutting the darkness like a knife.

There were a series of drops of blood, leading from the pool which had first attracted their attention, off into the dim distance at the side of the mighty building of the British Museum, which towered above them, like the ghost of some eastern castle.

"Follow this trail, Cunningham," said Shelley; "though I haven't much doubt of what we shall find at the end of it."

"What do you mean, sir?" asked Cunningham in awe-struck tones.

"Use your imagination, man," snapped Shelley. "Anyhow, you'll find out soon enough."

The drops of blood grew scarcer as they walked along. But Shelley, stooping at intervals, found that they also grew definitely fresher, as if they had been dropped more recently.

At one point there was again a little pool of blood. Someone had been badly wounded, that was obvious enough, and at this point he had doubtless paused to rest. The gruesome trail continued, however, and before long they arrived at the end of the road.

A man lay on his face before them. Sticking from his back was the hilt of a nasty-looking knife. Here was the source of the blood all right. Here was the man whose dreadful tracks they had been following around the forecourt of the British Museum. He was a tall man—over six feet in height—and his hair was iron-grey.

"What's the meaning of this?" asked Cunningham in puzzled tones. He was, he admitted to himself, both perturbed and scared.

Shelley grinned. Again it was not a pleasant grin, but this time it spoke volumes of relief. Cunningham thought it curious that his chief should be almost pleased that yet another murder had been committed.

"Has this got anything to do with our case?" he asked.

Again Shelley grinned. "That, my dear Cunningham," he said, indicating the body, "*is* our case."

"You mean…?" Cunningham paused.

"I mean," said Shelley, "that we have found the missing Dr. Crocker."

It was almost with relief that Cunningham set about the details of practical work which the preliminary stages of any murder case involve. He telephoned to Scotland Yard for a doctor, for finger-print experts, and for photographers. He assisted Shelley in a rapid examination of the body. It was still warm. The man had been dead only for a few minutes at most—which was clear enough, in any case, from the fact that the blood had still been in a semi-liquid condition when they had found it.

Soon the police cars came swinging up, and the astonished caretaker had to open wide the main gates of the British Museum to admit them—the first time for many years that they had been opened at such an incredible hour. The forecourt filled with activity, and the body of Dr. Crocker was taken into the main museum building for the doctor to make his examination.

"Not much need for me this time, Shelley," he said, when he had glanced at it.

"None at all, I imagine," answered Shelley. "Still, it's a formality that we have to go through. Some damned fool of a coroner would kick up a fuss if we didn't, anyway, and we have to observe all the rules."

"Well," said the doctor, after quite a perfunctory examination, "there's no doubt about how the poor devil died, anyhow. That stab penetrated right through, just grazing the heart."

"He would have lived for a short time afterwards, I suppose?" said Shelley.

"Oh, yes. He would be unconscious in three or four minutes," replied the doctor. "But before unconsciousness came on he'd probably be able to be quite active, able to walk and all that sort of thing, you know."

"He walked quite a considerable distance," said Shelley, and explained the way in which, together with Sergeant Cunningham, he had tracked the man across the forecourt.

The doctor nodded thoughtfully. "Yes," he said. "He'd bleed a good deal, of course. Still," he added in more cheerful tones, "this is one of the few cases in which there's none of that damned argument about *rigor mortis*. Why, the fellow's not been dead half an hour yet."

"No," said Shelley. "I can't think how the murderer got out."

There was a scurrying outside the door of the room in which they were talking, and Shelley hurriedly strode over to it.

"What the devil's all the row about?" he asked, and Cunningham hurried up to him.

"A most amazing thing, sir," he said.

"What is it?" asked Shelley.

"I've just seen someone in Great Russell Street, outside the railings, sir," he replied.

"That's not surprising," said Shelley. "After all, with all this activity going on, I expect we've got about half London walking about looking at us. It isn't every day that the curious-minded Cockney gets a chance of seeing Scotland Yard at work."

"Oh, but that isn't what I mean, sir," said Cunningham. "I saw a man connected with the case. He ran, and managed to get away before I was able to lay hands on him."

"Explain yourself," roared Shelley, quite losing patience at last. "Who is it that you saw in Great Russell Street, and allowed to get away from you?"

Cunningham lowered his voice to a suitable pitch of impressiveness. "Mr. Henry Baker," he said.

Chapter VIII

The Question of the Will

Shelley managed to snatch a few hours' sleep, and was up betimes the next morning. He splashed about in a cold bath, and then had a rub-down with a rough towel, this procedure being the best remedy he knew for making up for lack of sleep.

Then he went around to Scotland Yard, to face an equally tired and sleepy Cunningham.

"Look here, Cunningham," he said, "there's only one thing that strikes me about this case."

"Yes, sir," said Cunningham obediently, and waited for further instructions.

"There are so many threads that have to be followed up that I think we shall have to continue to work separately, and compare notes at the end of each day. How does that strike you?"

"Well," said Cunningham doubtfully, "if you think that I can tackle things on my own…"

"Of course you can," said Shelley, with a kindly smile. "You can question Mr. Moses Moss every bit as efficiently as I can myself."

"You think so, sir?" Cunningham still sounded a trifle doubtful, but felt none the less grateful for this praise from a quarter where praise was rare.

"And in the meantime," Shelley went on, considering that any reply to this question was unnecessary, "I think that I shall investigate the little question of the will of the late Professor Arnell."

"That certainly seems to be something that demands looking into, sir," Cunningham admitted.

"It certainly does," said Shelley. "If I am not sadly mistaken, that is going to provide the crux of the whole matter. Money is usually at the bottom of a murder case of this sort, and, if one finds the money motive, one can tell where to look for suspects."

"Good luck, anyhow, sir," said Cunningham with a smile.

"Same to you, Cunningham," said Shelley, "and I'm thinking that we shall need all the luck that's going, if we're to pull this thing off."

The office of Messrs. Samuel, Grant, and Samuel was high up in an office building in Chancery Lane—only a door or two away from an office which Shelley had frequently visited in connection with another murder case that he was investigating a year or two previously.

Mr. Samuel was a pleasant-looking young man, who swivelled around his revolving chair, and held out his hand frankly to Shelley.

"What can I do for you, Inspector?" he asked, a note of curiosity creeping into his voice.

"I want some information, sir," said Shelley, "which I think you can give me."

"If it's at all possible, Inspector, I will," replied the solicitor. "Always ready to assist in the work of you limbs of the law, you know."

He laughed, and Shelley felt more at home with him. The detective had a theory, which had up to the present invariably proved right, that a man's laugh was the most characteristic thing about him, and that it was possible to judge, according as to whether a man frankly guffawed or secretively sniggered, whether that man was of a good, dependable character or the direct opposite. As soon as he had heard the pleasant, deep-throated laugh of Mr. Samuel, he felt dead certain that this was a man to be trusted, a man in whose word one could place the most implicit confidence. And he proceeded accordingly, being sure that his instinct in this matter could not be at fault.

"It's about the death of Professor Arnell," he explained.

Samuel nodded. "I was expecting someone to come around about that matter, Inspector," he said.

"You knew he was dead?"

Samuel smiled. "I have my human weaknesses, Inspector," he said, "and one of them is that I like to read my morning paper at breakfast. I saw the professor's death reported in it, and guessed that there would be some sort of enquiry about it, since apparently he died suddenly."

"Not only," said Shelley, "did he die suddenly, Mr. Samuel—he died mysteriously."

"Mysteriously?" Samuel looked completely baffled, and then his face cleared up. "You mean suicide?"

Shelley shook his head solemnly. "No, sir," he said. "I mean—murder!"

"Good God!" Samuel bounced in his chair, sitting bolt upright in amazement, and staring at Shelley as if he were a ghost. "Who on earth would want to murder that poor harmless old fellow?"

"That," said Shelley somewhat sententiously, "is what I have to find out, if I can, and I am relying on you, Mr. Samuel, to help me."

"Of course I'll help you all I can," replied the solicitor, "though I don't see precisely what I can do."

"Well," Shelley explained, "first of all, have you any papers belonging to the old man here? If so, we might get a line on the motive and so on from them."

Samuel pressed a button on his desk, and a neat, businesslike typist appeared.

"Get out the box of documents belonging to Professor Arnell, will you, Miss Watkins?" directed the solicitor. "And bring them along here without delay."

"Yes, Mr. Samuel," said the girl, and retired once more to some inner sanctum where apparently she worked.

"Dreadful business," Samuel commented while she was away. "How did it happen?"

Shelley gave him a brief resumé of the circumstances of the crime, but without giving any indication of the general situation, or of the few facts which they had unearthed with regard to the possible identity of the murderer.

Soon, however, Miss Watkins had produced a steel box of documents, had placed it on the desk, together with a fearsome-looking heavy key, and had once more retired to her private office.

"You have the key as well as the box?" asked Shelley in some surprise.

"A duplicate," the solicitor explained, applying the key to the lock. "The Professor did not like the idea that it might be necessary to get a locksmith to break open the box. He was a very absent-minded old gentleman, and he thought that he might easily lose the key. So he had a duplicate one made, which we kept in the office here."

"Where was it kept?" asked Shelley, making a note of this state of affairs—for, he told himself, it might afterwards turn out to be important to know who had access to this box of documents.

"In the safe," replied the other, throwing back the lid of the box, and disclosing a mass of papers.

"Any possibility of anyone getting access to your safe?" pursued Shelley.

"Lord, no!" answered Samuel, horrified. "The stuff a lawyer keeps is pretty explosive, you know, Inspector. Doesn't do to take any risks, or let anyone know anything about it. Professional secrets and all that sort of thing, you see."

"I see," said Shelley, looking at the mass of papers with keen interest. "Now, what has he got there, that he leaves in your charge?"

"Oh," said the solicitor, with a shrug of his shoulders, "all the usual stuff, you know—deeds of houses, share certificates, copies of agreements made with publishers, and so on."

"Is his will there?"

"I don't know."

"You don't know?" Shelley was more than a trifle surprised at this. He had imagined that Arnell would certainly have left his will in charge of his lawyer.

"No." Samuel grinned. "Old Arnell was not a very trusting man in some respects. He didn't trust lawyers farther than he could see them, anyhow. We didn't make his will. I don't even know if he made one."

"Queer," said Shelley.

"Not so queer as you might think. After all—although this is an entirely unprofessional thing to say—making a will is a perfectly easy, straightforward business if you aren't aiming at any silly, complicated way of leaving your money. A lawyer is really necessary only if you want to tie your cash up in some complex fashion. And I imagine that Arnell would leave it all to his daughter. She's his only relative, as far as I'm aware. And he could easily make that will himself."

"I see," said Shelley. "Well, just glance through that collection of documents, will you? After all, the will might be there. You never know, do you?"

"Okay," said the lawyer, and turned out the contents of the box on to his desk.

One by one he went through the documents that it contained, examining each with some care, and then placing them in a neat pile by his side. At the end of this performance, when all the documents had been dealt with in turn, he leaned back in his chair with a sigh, and shook his head mournfully.

"No go, I'm afraid," he said.

"Not there, eh?" Shelley was gravely disappointed, for he had counted on finding the will here.

"No. To tell the truth, I didn't expect to find it, Inspector. As I told you, Arnell was a queer old bird in many ways, and I thought it very unlikely that he would leave the will in my care."

"Where do you think we should be likely to find it?" asked Shelley.

"Couldn't say," replied Samuel non-committally. Then his face lit up, as if a new idea had suddenly occurred to him. "D'you know," he said, "the old fellow had a safe deposit? Maybe his will would be there."

"That's highly probable, I should think," Shelley agreed. "Where is this safe deposit?"

"Not far from here. In the Chancery Lane place, you know. Is there any way of getting it open, I wonder? They're the very devil about getting anything out without the keys," explained the solicitor.

"Oh, I know all about that," said Shelley with a smile. "I've had to deal with them before. I think that I can manage that all right."

They walked around to the safe deposit, and, after a long talk with the manager, and a conversation over the 'phone with a personage very high up on the staff at Scotland Yard, Shelley managed to get permission to open the late Professor Arnell's safe, though only in the presence of the manager of the establishment, and another witness, Samuel agreeing to act in this capacity.

The keys turned, the neat little safe was opened, and the contents disclosed to view.

"Didn't I tell you he was a queer old bird?" murmured Samuel, as these things were taken out.

There were more share certificates and deeds of property. Apparently Professor Arnell had believed in taking no risks, preferring to have such of his property as might be either destroyed by fire or stolen by thieves spread in several places. That seemed the only explanation of this strange business of having some in his lawyer's office and some in the safe deposit.

But there were other things. Some scraps of old-fashioned jewellery—presumably his wife's—and something that made Shelley stare in open-eyed surprise. This was a photograph of a pleasant-looking young man of a Jewish cast of face. His hair was black, sleek, and shiny.

"I say," said Shelley, "would you object to my taking that photograph away with me? I feel that it may have a bearing on this case."

The manager of the safe deposit looked rather doubtful at the propriety of this course of action.

"Of course," Shelley added hastily, "I shall give you a receipt for it, and it will be returned later. In fact, if we have it long enough to photograph, and thus to make copies, that will do. I could return it to you tonight, if you feel doubtful about leaving it in my possession."

"Well, Inspector," said the manager, "it's just a little difficult. As you know, we have been breaking all the rules in allowing you to examine the contents of this safe at all. And I feel that I shouldn't allow anything from it to go out of our possession, you see." His voice tailed away into doubtful silence, and he looked at Shelley, obviously in some embarrassment at having to disagree with the great man from Scotland Yard.

"I tell you what I'll do," said Shelley. "I'll ring up the Yard, and get one of our photographers to come around here and photograph that picture. How will that suit you?"

"That certainly would be better," the manager admitted. "It is not that this picture is likely to be of any value, you know, but it is rather the principle of the thing. I hope that you understand me."

"That's all right," said Shelley briskly. "Now, what about this will?"

During this exchange of courtesies Samuel had been inspecting the documents with some care, and now he shook his head sadly.

"Afraid you're out of luck again, Inspector," he said. "The will's not here."

Shelley sighed. "That means another visit to Pinner, I suppose," he said. "A damned nuisance that this wasn't settled before, but it can't be helped."

So, with a word of gratitude to the manager, he left, and was soon bowling out towards Professor Arnell's house, which he had visited the night before.

Arrived there, he asked to see Miss Arnell, and was soon seated on the comfortable couch in her drawing-room, explaining his errand.

"I don't think," she said, "that father had any documents of that sort here, except those directly connected with his work."

"Still, you can't be sure," Shelley persisted. "And the will may help us to settle the problem of his death."

"All his papers are in the desk in his study," she went on, "and you are welcome, of course, to go through them if you care to do it. I'm afraid that you'll find it a most dreadful muddle," she went on with a smile. "Father was a terribly untidy man, and the one thing he was absolutely adamant about was that I was not to touch his private papers."

"That's all right," said Shelley, smiling in his turn. "We're quite accustomed to sorting out untidy masses of papers, you know, Miss Arnell. That's just part of our job, you see."

"I see. Then shall I take you along there?"

"If you don't mind."

Silently she led the way across the tiled hall into a cosy little study. It was lined with books almost from floor to ceiling, and before the window was a large roll-top desk—clearly the desk to which Miss Arnell had referred.

She fumbled in her handbag and produced a large bunch of keys. One of these she fitted to the lock of the desk, and, after some more fumbling, succeeded in turning it in the lock and opening the desk.

"There!" she said. The swing of her arm indicated the chaos which reigned. "A dreadful muddle" it was indeed, and Shelley groaned inwardly as he thought of the amount of work which this meant.

"Shall I leave you to it?" she asked.

"Well," said Shelley, "there doesn't really seem much point in your staying while I put all this in order. It looks as if it will be a longish job—take me a good hour to go through all that's there, I expect. And while I am about it I may as well go through it all. Even if the will isn't there, something else may give me some sort of pointer on the problem."

"Right," she said, with a graceful smile. "Just ring if there's anything that you want, won't you?"

"I will," said Shelley, and started on the job.

It was one of the most tiresome tasks that he had ever undertaken. Nearly all the papers in the desk were concerned in one way or another with the dead professor's work. There were memoranda of lectures delivered and listened to. There were notes of books read. There were letters received from editors of literary journals, from fellow-workers in the field of literary research, and from students in search of information. There were masses of notes on the various Elizabethan dramatists, and at least four separate beginnings to a book on the subject. Clearly the late Professor Arnell, whatever his merits as a student or a research-worker, was not in any way a tidy, methodical man. Yet every scrap of this documentary evidence had to be carefully sifted, every single piece of writing carefully scanned to see if it held any item of important information. Shelley knew too many cases where a detective had missed an invaluable clue by not being sufficiently thorough. He was thorough enough, yet, at the end of nearly two hours' solid work, he had to admit himself defeated. The will was not here. Nor was there any trace of any correspondence of a personal nature. Every letter dealt, in some way or another, with the late professor's work. It began to look as if Miss Arnell had been only too correct when she stated that her father had no friends apart from his literary companions.

Shelley sat back in his chair and thought deeply. That there would be a will somewhere he felt very certain. But where on earth could it be? He was sure that Professor Arnell was not the sort of man to die intestate. He had a good deal of money, and he was too fond of his daughter to run any risk of her not coming into her inheritance. The whole thing was baffling in the extreme.

The door opened slowly, and Miss Arnell's face peeped around it. There was a sparkle in her eye, and an air of suppressed excitement about her that instantly told Shelley that she had some important information to impart.

"Come in, Miss Arnell," he said.

She came in. "No luck, I suppose, Inspector," she said.

Shelley shook his head dolefully. "Not an atom of luck, I'm afraid," he admitted. "I'm sure your father must have made a will. And yet I can't find it anywhere. And there isn't a trace of any sort of personal correspondence here, either. It's all things connected with his work."

"That is to be expected," she said. "Father never did make friends easily. He always said that his work was his circle of friends. And he had no desire to become friendly with anyone who couldn't argue learnedly about Marlowe and Peele and Greene and all the others."

"But what is it that you want to tell me?" asked Shelley suddenly. He could see that she was simply bursting with information, and it might well be that this information was of some value.

"How did you know…?" she began, and then broke off. "It's only that I have found father's will," she said.

"*You've* found his will?" Shelley was frankly incredulous. "Where on earth did you find it?"

"In a letter."

"What letter?" Shelley could be laconic enough when the occasion demanded it.

"A letter that has just come by post. Look." She held it out to him—a registered letter, posted in London (Holborn Sub-office). He found himself noting this automatically as he drew the document from its envelope.

"Who sent it?" he asked.

She shook her head helplessly. "I haven't the least idea," she said.

"Was there any covering letter with it?" he asked.

She shook her head again. "No. It was quite by itself in the envelope. I can't think who can have sent it to me, or why."

"Do you recognise the writing?" asked Shelley.

"No." The envelope was addressed in a crude, uneducated scrawl, which might, as Shelley at once realised, be merely a disguised hand.

"Have you read it?"

She nodded.

"Don't mind if I do so?"

"Of course not," she said. "After all, you said it was important, and now that we have found it I want you to read it without delay."

Shelley read the document aloud. "This is the last will and testament of me, Julius Arnell, Professor Emeritus in the University of Portavon. I hereby give and bequeath all my property to my daughter, Violet Arnell, for her sole use during her lifetime. At her death it is to go, whether she has issue or not, to my nephew, Moses Moss, to belong to him and his heirs and assigns, absolutely."

She smiled a tremulous smile. "Just like him, I think," she said. "Although he was so untidy and impractical in some things, in all the things that really mattered, he would have everything just correct."

"H'm." Shelley was not altogether satisfied. "You think it's like the sort of will that you would have expected your father to make?"

"Yes." She was quite emphatic on that point.

"Well, that's all right," said Shelley, and glanced at the will again. Then he whistled softly to himself.

"What's the matter?" Violet Arnell sensed that he was suddenly surprised and uneasy about something.

"Look at this again," commanded Shelley.

She looked. "I don't see anything curious," she said.

"Then you probably don't know that Professor Wilkinson died in the British Museum some six months ago, and that Dr. Crocker was stabbed there last night," said Shelley.

"How dreadful!" She was horrified, and yet puzzled at the same time.

"But I don't see…" she murmured.

"Take another look at your father's will," Shelley commanded.

"At the will?" There was still a tone of puzzlement in her voice, but she obediently picked up the document and read it through with the utmost care, as if resolved that now whatever peculiar circumstance had struck Shelley should not escape her eager scrutiny.

"But I still don't see…" she said again.

"Look at it once more," commanded the detective. "If you don't see it then, I shall have to explain it to you. But somehow I fancy that you will realise what I'm getting at in a moment."

She looked. Then she uttered a little scream of terror. "Professor Wilkinson," she said. "Dr Crocker."

"Yes," said Shelley sternly. "I don't know what it means. It doesn't seem to make sense somehow. But Professor Wilkinson, who died at the British Museum six months ago, and Dr. Crocker, who died there last night, are the witnesses of your father's will!"

Chapter IX

Moses Moss, Esquire

While Shelley was thus chasing a somewhat elusive document, Cunningham was on the trail of an almost equally
elusive gentleman. He had felt highly honoured that his
chief was giving him so much independent work to do, for
this was the first big murder case in which he had pursued
investigations of anything like this importance on his own.
Yet, before the end of the morning, he began to wonder if
an honour which involved so much work was really worth
while, after all.

First of all, since young Baker had given him to understand that Moss lived somewhere in Bloomsbury, he made
his way to the Tottenham Court Road Police Station, and
was soon in close confabulation with the inspector in charge.

"Know a young fellow called Moses Moss?" he asked, as
soon as he had introduced himself, and had chatted for a
few minutes in order to get on friendly terms.

"Why, what's young Moss been doing to attract the attention of the Yard?" asked the inspector in surprised tones.

"So you do know him?"

"Yes," answered the inspector willingly. "Know him professionally, as you might say."

"A crook?"

"Oh, nothing like that. There was some sort of burglary at his flat in Great Russell Street a week or two ago. Clumsy affair, and we caught the chap next day. But young Moss got the wind up properly about it," explained the inspector. "Said everybody might be murdered in their beds, and all that sort of thing. You know what hysterical people say when they think that the man who robbed 'em isn't being arrested quickly enough to suit their convenience."

Cunningham made sympathetic noises, and awaited further revelations. The revelations did not show much sign of coming, so he asked for the number of the house in which Mr. Moss had his flat, and received it.

"There's a fellow there in charge—sort of janitor-caretaker," the inspector explained. "If you're checking up on the young fellow's movements I should think he'll be able to put you on the right track."

"Thanks very much," said Cunningham. "That's just the sort of fellow that I want to get hold of."

He rose to go, and then another idea came into his head.

"What sort of chap is this Moss?" he asked. "Decent fellow?"

"Very decent," returned the other. "Bit highly strung, I fancy. That's about all that's the matter with him. I should imagine that you'd find him easy enough to deal with—that is, if you can get hold of him. He seems to keep the most unearthly hours."

"That sounds cheerful," was Cunningham's comment. And, before the day was done, he was to learn that his comment was abundantly justified.

He went around, first of all, to the flat in Great Russell Street, to find, as he had anticipated, that Mr. Moss had already gone out for the day. However, he found the janitor-caretaker in a little office at the entrance to the block of flats. He was a garrulous little Cockney, short and fat, and Cunningham at once realised that, if any information was obtainable, there would be but little difficulty in getting it out of him. The difficulty, indeed, would rather be to stem the flow of reminiscence when once it was properly started on its headlong career.

"Moss?" he said with a cheery smile. "Why, yus, guv'nor, I knows Mr. Moss all right. A nicer young chap you never did meet."

Cunningham rightly diagnosed this as indicating a ready hand with tips, and discounted its value accordingly. He made further questions force their way into the conversation, and soon obtained some information which might, or might not, prove useful in due course.

"Last night. Now let me see," said the caretaker, pursing up his lips thoughtfully. "Last night I lef' this 'ere orfice at ar'-pas' twelve. He hadn't come in up to then, not so far as I remember."

"Half-past twelve? Do you have to work as late as that?" asked Cunningham, knowing that a little human sympathy goes a long way in establishing a more friendly footing.

"Yus. I works all hours 'ere. 'Tis about time they put things on a proper footin'. I tells the landlord that every week or two, but 'e don't tike no notice. So I just sticks to me job and 'opes for the best."

"Is Mr. Moss a pretty gay dog, then?" pursued Cunningham, leading the conversation back into what he hoped would be more profitable channels.

"Ho, yus!" the caretaker chuckled. "Out 'alf the night, 'e is, sometimes. Though we must all 'ave our bit of fun, you know. After all, we're only young once, guv'nor. We all 'ave our fling in our time."

"That's right." Cunningham agreed. "But it's rather important that I should get hold of him as soon as I can. Any idea of where he'd be now?"

"Regent Street," said the caretaker. "That's where he'd be. Yus. Regent Street."

"Where in Regent Street?" asked Cunningham, and the old Cockney chuckled again.

"Couldn't tell you, guv'nor," he said. "'E works in a motor shop in Regent Street, selling cars to them toffs up in the West End. That's all I knows about 'im."

"Don't know the name of the firm, I suppose?"

"Sorry, guv'nor, I don't. If I did, I'd tell you, strite I would."

"Right. That's all I can do, I suppose," said Cunningham, and then, another idea suddenly striking him, he added: "I suppose you know that he *did* come home last night, don't you?"

"Ho, yus," said the caretaker. "I know 'e come 'ome, all right. I seen 'im this morning, seen 'im with me own eyes. 'Mornin', Bill,' 'e says to me as 'e goes out, so cheerful as you like. I will say that for Mr. Moss, it don't matter 'ow thick a night 'e may 'ave 'ad, 'e always 'aves a cheery word for me next mornin'."

"Good," said Cunningham. "Thanks very much." And, pressing a half-crown into the not unwilling hand of the old Cockney, he made a hurried escape before another instalment of gossip could be poured into his ear.

In Regent Street he found that his task was by no means easy. There were not many car dealers in Regent Street itself, but he knew that the name of the street might well be an elastic term, and in the smaller streets running off the principal thoroughfare there seemed to be such shops by the dozen. He tried each in turn, valiantly working along from the Oxford Circus end of the street, and drawing a blank at each one. Some of the managers looked at him in amazement, but most of them were quite courteous, announcing that, though they had no one named Moss on their staff, it was possible that one of their competitors a little farther along might know more about him.

It was all very trying. Although they all did their best to be helpful, Cunningham was getting almost desperate, and was thinking that the elusive Mr. Moss had lied to the caretaker of the block of Bloomsbury flats, and was really engaged in some other—perhaps some less respectable—profession, when he struck oil at last.

It was in a shabby little side-street, near the Piccadilly Circus end of Regent Street, that he at last ran his quarry to earth, though even here he did not find him at once.

"Moses Moss?" said the manager. "Yes; he works here."

"Could I have a word with him?" asked Cunningham.

"You can when he comes in," answered the manager.

"What, hasn't he arrived yet?" asked Cunningham.

"Oh, yes," replied the manager with a superior smile; "he came in at the usual hour this morning, but he's off on a job. He's taking a client for a trial run in a car, you see—the sort of thing that clients want, these days," he added ruefully, "and if they don't get a damned good run we don't get any money."

"I see," agreed Cunningham. "But when do you think there's any chance of his coming back? It's very important that I should get hold of him as soon as possible."

"Yes?" The manager looked at him with an air of some curiosity. "Money troubles, eh?"

"No." Cunningham smiled. "Nothing like that. Just a bit of information that I think he can give me. So when do you think that I shall be able to get him?"

"Not for some time," was the unwelcome reply. "Not for some hours, anyway. When Moss gets a client on the string he usually takes some hours before he gets anywhere with him. And, as likely as not, he'll have lunch with the fellow and then take him around to Sally's for a drink afterwards, just to mark the bargain, as you might say."

"Sally's? Is that the club in St. Martin's Lane?" asked Cunningham.

"That's right. Dull little show, I call it. Can't think why so many people go there," replied the manager. "Still, it seems to do pretty good business, all right, and I know that Moss goes there nearly every day—certainly every day that he's got a client on the string."

"What time is he likely to be there?" asked Cunningham.

"Not till three o'clock, 'cos that's when the club opens," sniggered the manager. "And I haven't the least idea where he'll be between now and then, because, you see, we don't keep very close tabs on our men. As long as they bring home the bacon, that's all that really matters. They can do it as they damn' well like."

"Nuisance," was Cunningham's comment. "That means that I've got some hours to waste."

"'Fraid it does. Only sorry that I can't help you any more. Still, you see the way it is. I haven't the least idea where the man is now."

"Oh, that's all right. Good morning," said Cunningham.

"Cheerio," returned the manager.

Cunningham spent a miserable morning, drinking coffee and wasting as much time over it as possible. Then, when the time for lunch arrived, he lingered over his frugal meal as long as he dared, glancing miserably at the clock at frequent intervals, and cursing the laggard minutes which dragged so heavily by. Eventually, however, the hour of three approached, and he thankfully paid his bill and wended his way towards St. Martin's Lane.

Sally's Club was not far from the London Coliseum, and was reached by some dark and winding stairs. The club was at the top of a high and ramshackle building, and when Cunningham tapped on the door a grille opened, and a female face peered out at him suspiciously.

"Yes?" snapped the owner of the face, frowning at the intruder portentously, as if trying to remember under what unpleasant conditions she had formerly seen him.

"I want to see Mr. Moss," said Cunningham in as coaxing a tone as he could command.

"Well, he's not here," she snapped and banged the grille to with an emphatic gesture.

Cunningham tapped again and the grille opened.

"I'll come in and wait," he announced.

"You'll do nothing of the kind. This is a private club, and only members and their friends are admitted."

"Well, I'm Mr. Moss's friend, and I'll wait and see him."

"Then you can wait on the stairs."

"Wait a moment," said Cunningham, and produced his warrant card. "How does that strike you?" he asked. "Now, perhaps you'll let me in."

The hard, unfeminine face, glaringly white with powder, the lips a vivid slash of red across its clear whiteness, seemed to relent. "Very well, Sergeant," said Sally—for she it was— "I'll let you in. Can't do anything else, I suppose. But you'll realise, I hope, that I can't go having any damned stranger who says he's a friend of a member wandering in without as much as a 'by your leave.'"

"I understand. That's all right," said Cunningham, and was forthwith admitted.

The club was quite a small place. At one end of it was a bar around which a few men were standing, glasses of beer in hands. Behind the bar were bottles of wine and spirits and two barrels of beer. In the room itself were a few wicker chairs, occupied by languid-looking women, and a table on which their glasses were resting. In one corner was a mechanical "pintable" at which two or three people were playing. On the wall was a dart-board. And that was all. The place was obviously merely a drinking-den, a place by which a group of people were enabled to get drinks at hours during which a benevolent government had seen fit to close the public houses, and Cunningham, knowing the habits of such places, was vaguely surprised to think that there had been difficulty in getting in. Usually, he reflected, a place of this type would make anyone a member without further argument. But possibly the woman had realised that he was a police officer, and so paraded this ridiculous show of caution to impress him. Anyhow, whatever the reason for the difficulty, he had now overcome it, and, ordering a glass of beer at the bar, he sat down on a vacant chair to await the arrival of Moses Moss.

He had not long to wait, as it happened, for, long before he had finished his glass of beer—incidentally finding it of an inferior brew—a young man came in.

"Someone here to see you, Mr. Moss," said Sally, and made a mute gesture in Cunningham's direction. Moss looked at him with a puzzled expression on his face.

"Want to see me?" he asked, approaching Cunningham, his countenance still screwed up in an air of bewilderment.

"But who are you? I don't know you," Moss objected. "And what do you want with me?"

"Information," answered Cunningham, and lowered his voice to a tactful murmur. "I'm an officer from Scotland Yard and I want to have a chat."

"Scotland Yard?" Was it mere fancy, Cunningham asked himself, or did this young man definitely wince at the mention of police headquarters?

"Yes," he answered aloud. "I am investigating the death of the late Professor Arnell."

"I saw he was dead," answered Moss. "Saw it in the paper. But what's that got to do with me?"

"Wasn't he a relative of yours?"

"Oh, yes," admitted Moss. "He was my uncle. But I never saw much of him. In fact, I think that when my mother married my father she was more or less cut off by her family—I think that they had some sort of prejudice against the Jews, you know, and did not like the idea of her marrying into a Jewish household. This is all surmise, for she never spoke to me of it, but I summed things up that way."

"Would you be surprised to know that he left money to you?" asked Cunningham, and Moss grinned.

"I certainly should," he said. "The old devil never did anything for me in his lifetime, and I shouldn't expect him to do anything for me after his death."

"Well," said Cunningham, not knowing, of course, what the disclosure of the will might bring forth, and in any case not wishing to give away any information, but thinking that this might prove a useful lever to extract the data that he needed, "I can't give you any information about that, but we understand that you may benefit under his will."

"Hope to God I do," answered Moss. "I'm pretty well broke at the moment, old man, and I don't mind admitting it. So the old fellow has turned up trumps after all, has he?"

"Don't go counting too certainly on that, sir," Cunningham advised him. "I only told you that it was at any rate possible."

"I imagine that your 'possible' is as good as another man's 'certain,'" returned the other, and Cunningham let the matter rest at that.

"There's another point," he said, "that has to be settled—purely as a matter of form. This is a question that we have to ask everyone who might be connected with the case, or who might be expected to benefit by Professor Arnell's death."

"Carry on," said Moss. "You won't offend me, whatever your question is. I'm not one of these thin-skinned devils who take offence at every question."

"Can you give me an account of your movements yesterday?" asked Cunningham.

Moss whistled softly. "Alibis, eh?" he said, and Cunningham nodded.

"You will understand that it is important to trace the alibis of everyone in any way connected with the case," he explained, although he reflected that the explanation was probably quite unnecessary.

"Let me see, now," Moss said thoughtfully. "What exactly did I do? Oh, yes, I know. I went to the British Museum in the morning."

Cunningham was unable to restrain the "What?" that sprung unbidden to his lips.

"Yes," said Moss. "The British Museum. What's wrong with that? Nothing unlawful about going to look at the Egyptian antiquities, is there? I happen to be interested in ancient Egypt, and I went along there to have a look at them. O.K.?"

"O.K.," said Cunningham. "What time were you in the British Museum?"

"From about eleven o'clock until half-past twelve, I should think," answered Moss. "I had had a thickish night the night before, and I didn't have breakfast until after ten."

"What did you do when you left the Museum?" pursued Cunningham.

"Went to my firm's place off Regent Street," answered the young Jew. "There was an old lady there who was trying to decide whether she wanted a car or not. I ran her out to

Slough and back—along the Great West Road—had tea with her, and succeeded in landing the sale at about half-past six."

"Then?" Cunningham was resolved to leave nothing to chance, although he felt fairly sure that the crucial part of the alibi would lie in the time which the young man had spent at the British Museum.

"Then I went home, had some dinner in my flat, and went to my pub—the Fifteen Swords in Bloomsbury Street—where I played shove-ha'penny until closing time. Then to bed, as old Pepys used to say."

"What parts of the day have you any sort of alibi for?" asked Cunningham. "I mean, what times have you any confirmation for?"

Again the young man plunged deep in thought. "The British Museum part I think I can confirm," he said. "I had a chat with the curator of the Egyptian Antiquities Room. A friend of mine has been doing some excavations in Luxor, and some of his stuff was on show there. He asked me to go and make enquiries about what they were doing. I think that fellow will know me, and will remember my being there."

"And the rest of the day?"

"Well, the old lady—Mrs. Hatton, of Slough—will bear me out for the period from one-thirty until six or so, the waiter fellow at the flats where I live will give you the time I had dinner, and the barman at the pub, as well as some of the 'regulars' there, will give you my times for the evening," announced the young man. "I don't think, in fact, that there will be any difficulty for any part of the day. I think my alibi, my dear old chap, is about as watertight as it can be."

"Seems quite satisfactory," said Cunningham, putting into his voice far more conviction than he really felt.

"Anything more?" asked Moss, obviously getting restive under this cross-examination.

"Not much," Cunningham admitted. "Only the names and addresses of the people concerned."

"By Jove, you fellows are pretty thorough, aren't you?" said Moss, in open admiration.

"Have to be in our job, sir," said Cunningham, and wrote down the names and addresses that the young man gave him.

"And now," said Moss, when the work was apparently complete, "am I free to go where I like?"

"Perfectly free, sir," said Cunningham, "although I should like you if you happen to leave London, to let us know where we can get hold of you. You are an important person in this case, you see, and we just can't afford to lose touch with you."

"Right-ho," Moss answered. "I'll take care to do that. And that really is all?"

"That," Cunningham said, "really is all."

As he was about to leave the club, now rapidly filling up, Moss called him back.

"Might I be permitted to ask you one question, old man?" he asked.

"If you want to, fire away," answered Cunningham. "Although, mind you," he added cautiously, "I can't guarantee to answer it. That must depend on my judgment."

"Oh, of course, I understand that," said Moss, with a smile. "Official secrecy and all that sort of thing. That's understood, of course; that goes without saying. Oh, yes, certainly."

Cunningham was rather puzzled at this indecision of Moss. The young man seemed uneasy and on edge, as if there were a question on the tip of his tongue, a question which he was longing to ask, but which, none the less, he did not dare to risk putting to the test.

"Well," he said, at length, when Moss seemed to have talked himself to a standstill, so to speak, and did not show any inclination to ask this question, whatever it might be, "what is this question that you want to ask me?"

"Why," asked Moss, "were you so surprised when I said that I'd been at the British Museum yesterday?"

"Do you mean to say you don't know?" asked Cunningham. Moss shook his head mutely.

"You said you read in the papers of Professor Arnell's death," Cunningham went on.

"That's right," said Moss.

"Didn't your paper mention where he died?"

"No. Or if so, I didn't notice it."

"He died," said Cunningham slowly, "in the Reading Room of the British Museum."

Before he left Sally's Club the detective saw Moses Moss slowly walk towards the bar, his face a ghastly white, and order a double brandy.

Chapter X

An Appeal

Mr. Henry Fairhurst clicked his teeth in annoyance. "Dear, dear," he said mildly. "Now isn't that too annoying for words?"

Miss Fairhurst looked up from her book. "Isn't what annoying, Henry?" she asked. "I wish that you wouldn't make these ridiculous statements without at least trying to explain what they mean."

"Did I say that aloud?" asked her brother. "Really, Sarah, I wasn't aware that I spoke my thoughts. I was, to tell you the truth, only thinking aloud."

"If you think aloud, Henry," returned Miss Fairhurst, "you should be prepared to share your thoughts and make an effort at explaining them."

"I was merely thinking," said Henry, dutifully explaining—as requested, "that it was very annoying that Mr. Shelley did not invite me to help him over the case."

"Nonsense!" Miss Fairhurst could put a lot of healthy contempt into one word, especially when that word was accompanied by a snort of gargantuan proportions. "Do you imagine, Henry Fairhurst, that any single creature on God's earth thinks of you as a useful detective?"

Henry smiled deprecatingly, and gripped his pince-nez firmly before replying. "Well, one person does, at any rate, my dear," he said.

"What?" His sister sat bolt upright in her chair, and regarded him with an air of complete astoundment. "Who, may I ask?"

"One of the principal witnesses in this case," he said, "rang up this afternoon while you were out shopping, my dear Sarah, and asked if she might come around to discuss the case with me."

"*She?*" Sarah pounced on the most important word in the sentence. "Who is this hussy, I should like to know?"

"Miss Arnell," explained Henry. He was somewhat fearful, it must be admitted. This was the first time that he had dared to do such a thing as bringing a young woman to the house, and he was not at all certain of what would be the outcome of it. Sarah was a curious creature, the workings of whose mind he had never succeeded in fathoming, but he was sure that this would be a matter for fireworks of one kind or another. And he was not mistaken.

"Miss Arnell, indeed!" exclaimed Sarah. "And who, pray, is Miss Arnell?"

"The daughter of the man I saw murdered in the Museum Reading Room," explained Henry, feeling more like a worm with each moment that passed.

"And when have you taken the liberty of inviting her to my house?" asked his sister, magnificently disregarding the fact that the house and its contents were actually Henry's own property.

"This evening," Henry faltered. "In fact," he went on, as the outer bell rang, "in fact, I—er—I should think that is her at the door now."

Miss Fairhurst set her face grimly and looked towards the door as Miss Arnell entered. Nor did that young lady's charm and sweetness do anything to alter the steady determination on Miss Fairhurst's countenance. She was clearly resolved to preserve her dignity and yet, at the same time, to study the young lady at close quarters. Although she said nothing to express such an opinion, both Henry Fairhurst and his visitor felt sure that his sister was mentally asking herself if the young lady could, by any possibility, be a parricide.

"This is Miss Arnell, my dear," said Henry nervously. "And this, Miss Arnell, is my sister, Miss Fairhurst."

"How do you do, Miss Fairhurst?" said Violet Arnell, holding out her hand to the grim old gorgon and smiling her most winning smile.

"Uh," said Miss Fairhurst, taking the hand in her own for a moment, and then dropping it again as if it had been red hot.

"Won't you sit down?" said Henry, still nervous, but feeling that, with every moment that passed, he was getting a better control of the situation, difficult though that situation still was.

"Thank you," she said gratefully, and sank into the depths of a cosy arm-chair.

"And now," Henry went on, "can you tell me what I can do for you, Miss Arnell?"

She shuffled a little in her chair. She was plainly ill at ease. Whatever her request might be, she seemed to be finding it difficult to put into words. She made one or two attempts to speak, and then, with a plaintive smile, gulped, and began again.

"I understand, Mr. Fairhurst," she said at last, "that you know a good deal about this case."

"Huh!" Sarah grunted contemptuously, but Henry, taking his courage in both hands, disregarded her interruption and devoted himself to replying to Miss Arnell's question.

"I know a certain amount about it," he said modestly. "You see, I happen to have seen your father just before his unfortunate death, Miss Arnell. And I happen to have been the person who was able to discover that Dr. Wilkinson, of Northfield University, died in somewhat similar circumstances some months ago."

"I understood that from the papers," she said. "It was that that made me ring you up, Mr. Fairhurst. I just looked your name up in the telephone book. Oh, you must help me!"

"Of course I will," he replied earnestly. "But what is it that you want me to do? And, in any case, why are you so upset? I know that this death of your father is a very dreadful thing…but why the sudden upset feeling now? Why did you ring me up today?"

Violet Arnell looked him straight in the face. Her eyes brimmed over with tears, and her mouth set in a hard line. The effort of keeping her composure was clearly a troublesome one. Then she spoke, pronouncing each word separately, with a distinct pause between each, as if she found the very act of articulation difficult.

"They…arrested…Harry…Baker…today," she said.

While Henry was still puzzling over this statement he saw a surprising thing. He saw Sarah's face dissolve into a sudden unwonted kindness, and he saw Sarah swiftly rise from her chair, and go towards Violet Arnell. His sister turned her head in his direction, and spoke in a strange, clipped voice.

"Go into the kitchen quickly," she said. "Open the cupboard on the left of the gas-oven, and get out that bottle of brandy. Quick, man! Don't stand there like a ninny. Do what I tell you."

There was such an air of masterful determination about her that Henry went without hesitation. What she wanted with brandy he could not think. But then Henry, as should by this time be clear enough, did not really understand feminine human nature.

When he returned with the brandy and a tumbler Sarah took the bottle and glass from him without a word, poured out a good stiff dose, and gave it to Violet Arnell.

"There, my dear," she said. "You'll feel better when you've put that away."

Without a word Violet Arnell took the proffered glass, and gulped off the pungent spirit, not without a good deal of coughing and spluttering in the process.

"Ah," she said, "that's much better, thanks." She smiled gratefully at them both.

"I thought so," said Miss Fairhurst, with a satisfied grin. All her disapproval seemed to have vanished in this little effort of restoration. "You were on the verge of fainting. I had to get this fool of a brother of mine to get some brandy for you."

"Silly of me," said Miss Arnell, smiling wistfully again. "I'm sorry. But, you see, I felt so hopeless about Harry. You will help me, won't you?"

"Of course he will," remarked Sarah, taking her brother's permission for granted. "Of course he'll do all he can to help you. And he's not such a fool as all that, really, although he does act like a perfect idiot sometimes."

"Don't you think," Henry interjected nervously, "that it would be a good idea if Miss Arnell told us what it's all about? Except that they arrested Harry Baker—and I don't even know who Harry Baker is—I've learnt nothing at all since Miss Arnell came in."

"Of course," she said suddenly. "I didn't tell you anything, did I? So foolish of me."

"Well," said Henry and waited.

Violet Arnell took herself firmly in hand and began. "Harry Baker," she said, "is my fiancé. We have been engaged for some months now. But my father strongly disapproved of the engagement. He said that he wouldn't see me marrying a penniless young schoolmaster. He thought that I should aim at someone a little higher on the social scale. Father," she added, "was a rather old-fashioned man. A good crusted old Tory, someone once called him, and I'm afraid that it was a pretty good description of him."

Henry made sympathetic noises and waited again.

"Father went as far as to say that if I married Harry he'd cut me out of his will, and leave all his money to a queer cousin of mine—a man called Moses Moss," she went on.

"But what about your fiancé's arrest?" asked Henry. "You see, that provides him with an excellent motive, if I may say so, for murdering your father. But the police don't work on motive alone, you know. They want proof of opportunity to commit a crime. And in this case there are two crimes."

"Three," corrected his sister, and read from the newspaper before her an account of the death of Dr. Crocker, which had taken place the night before. Henry looked at her aghast.

"You see," went on Violet Arnell, "it's not merely that Harry had a reason for putting father out of the way. He inherited some money from Dr. Wilkinson, who was a distant relative of his. That was what put the police on his track, I think."

"Even so," murmured Henry thoughtfully, "that's no real reason why he should be arrested. Motive in the two cases would not be enough alone. They must have more to go on than that."

"They have," Violet explained somewhat grimly. "Harry was outside the British Museum last night, at the time when the murder was committed."

"Good Lord!" Henry Fairhurst did not often permit himself the use of strong language of this sort, but he felt that this was a privileged occasion.

"How on earth," he asked, when he had recovered his equanimity, "was he such a fool as to venture there last night?"

"That's really what I've come to you about, Mr. Fairhurst," replied the girl. "Last night Harry was going to see me. After he had finished correcting some examination papers at school he had promised to call around and see me. But while I was at tea a note from him was brought round by one of the boys. This is it." She fumbled in her handbag and produced a letter which she passed over to Mr. Fairhurst, who, conscious that his sister was craning her neck in a vain effort to peer over his shoulder and read it, proceeded to read its contents aloud.

"Dear Violet," the note said, "I'm afraid that I shan't be able to come tonight. I've received a most mysterious missive, telling me to be outside the British Museum from midnight onwards. It hints that there will be developments with regard to the death of your father. I suspect that the police are going to try out something. Anyhow, my dear, I must be there, so I'm going straight up to town when school ends. Will give you a ring in the morning and tell you all about it. Wish me luck. Love. Harry."

"You see, Miss Fairhurst?" said Violet. "It must have been some sort of trap. Oh, who can this villain be? Why has he such a grudge against Harry?" She was on the verge of tears, and Sarah, again much to her brother's surprise, made her way across the room to the girl's side and patted her hand sympathetically.

"Never you mind, my dear," she said. "Henry will do something for you, and for your young man, too. Won't you, Henry?"

Henry, plunged deep in a daydream in which he out-witted Scotland Yard as well as the cleverest brains in the underworld, roused himself to reply.

"I'll do my best," he announced, and Violet Arnell bright-ened up immediately.

"First of all," he added, "can you tell me if the original of this letter is anywhere to be had, Miss Arnell? I mean, of course, the note that was used to lure your fiancé to the neighbourhood of the British Museum last night. After all, if he's to put up any sort of defence, it is essential that it should be found. Otherwise, his explanation of why he was there will sound very weak, very weak indeed."

"I don't know," Miss Arnell replied. "You see, I haven't seen Harry since…since his arrest."

"Well, that's the first thing to be seen to, anyway," remarked Henry with an air of intense resolution. "And then there is the matter of his inheritance from Dr. Wilkinson. Did he expect that, or was it a bolt from the blue, so to speak? Do you happen to know anything at all about it, Miss Arnell? It would certainly be most helpful if you could tell me anything about it."

"A complete bolt from the blue, I think," she announced. "I know that Harry was both surprised and delighted at the legacy. He said that he hadn't even known that Dr. Wilkinson was related to him, not to mention the expectation of a legacy from him."

"That's a useful point, anyhow," replied Henry, and then paused, deep in thought once more.

"I don't think," he announced at length, "that there is much that I can do here. I think that I shall have to go to Scotland Yard and see if they can help me at all. After all, I've been of some use to them in this case. I've been able to provide them with some good information, and, if I tell them that I am acting on your behalf, I am sure that they will be pleased to tell me what is being done, and what are the grounds for their arrest of Mr. Baker."

"Would you do that for me, Mr. Fairhurst?" asked Violet Arnell, her voice plaintively pleading her case. "If you would, I should be so grateful. You see, I have no one now that father is dead and Harry is arrested. I know that Harry can't be guilty of these horrible crimes, but I feel so completely helpless. There seems to be nothing that I can do."

"That's all right, my dear," interjected Sarah gruffly. "We'll do everything we can to help you. We'll get the rogue who's responsible for all this. Never worry."

"I think," Henry announced, "that I'll go straight up to Scotland Yard now."

"Do," said his sister. "There's no time to be lost. Take a taxi, Henry."

This was a new attitude with a vengeance. Sarah had always suggested that anything more expensive than a bus or a tube train would be ruinously extravagant. But Henry was rapidly learning that the Sarah he had known all his life was not necessarily the real Sarah, after all.

"Only one thing," he said, as he struggled into his over-coat, and wound an old-fashioned muffler of the type known as a "comforter" around his neck. "Don't expect sudden results. We may not land our fish too quickly, you know. We're fishing in deep waters."

How deep the waters were he little guessed.

Chapter XI

The Exhumation

"My dear Mr. Fairhurst," said Shelley in some irritation, "you surely can't expect me to go further than that. I have told you that I feel tolerably sure that Mr. Baker is guilty—he would not have been arrested without thoroughly good grounds. Scotland Yard is not in the habit of arresting innocent men."

Henry looked pained. "I was not, my dear Inspector," he moaned, "suggesting that Scotland Yard was in the habit of doing anything so dreadful. But I was suggesting that mistakes occur, and that this was one of the mistakes."

"If you think so, my dear sir," returned Shelley, "my advice to you is: Go on and prove it! Other people have tried to do that, but not many of them have found themselves able to beat the Yard at its own game. If you think you can—well, good luck to you! But don't expect any help from us."

"But I *do* expect some help from you," Henry complained. "If I am going to set to work to find a murderer, Inspector, I have to possess all the necessary data. That is only reasonable, surely."

Shelley grinned. "Daniel in the den of lions isn't in it, Mr. Fairhurst," he said. "An amateur in the den of professionals.

Very well; in view of the fact that you have been good enough to give us some exceedingly useful information, I will allow you to know just a little of what is being done by us—but on one condition."

"And that is…?" Henry was all eagerness now. To tell the truth, this was more than he had dared to hope, even in his most optimistic moments.

"That is, my dear sir, that anything which you may learn in the course of this little agreement of ours shall be kept as the strictest of secrets; in other words, that no one—no one at all, mind you—shall hear anything which may be divulged to you here. This is all quite unofficial, of course, and I am only doing it because I think that there may just possibly be something in what you say, and you have already shown some evidence of wisdom in this business of criminology."

"Inspector!" Henry's voice was quivering, his pince-nez trembling perilously on his absurd nose.

"First," said Shelley, affecting not to notice the little man's emotion, "you will have what I imagine is a new experience for you, my dear sir."

"Yes?"

"Yes."

"What is it?" Henry could not resist the direct question.

"You will have the opportunity of attending an exhumation."

"Who is being exhumed?" exclaimed Henry in some surprise.

"Use your brains, my dear Mr. Fairhurst. Who do you think it could be?" Shelley could be almost rude when he desired, and his more brutal instincts occasionally seemed to come to the surface when dealing with the mild-mannered little Henry Fairhurst.

Henry thought deeply for a moment, his brow wrinkled in the effort of mental concentration. Then his face cleared up, and he looked at the detective and smiled gently.

"Of course, it is quite obvious," he said.

"Quite," said Shelley in return, still waiting for Henry's decision.

"Professor Wilkinson, of course."

"Of course."

So soon they were bowling along in a huge police car, bound for the cemetery outside London where Professor Wilkinson had been buried some months earlier. In the car with them were Sergeant Cunningham and an official from the Home Office, the permission of the Home Secretary having been obtained, as is necessary for all exhumations, which are granted only if the most urgent need is proved by the police authorities.

At the cemetery a mournful little group greeted them. There were two burly men armed with spades, and one of the cemetery officials, who frowned disapprovingly on the whole proceeding, as if he thought it an unnecessary insult to the concern under his charge that this deed should be done.

It was a pitch-black night, and in the light of two swinging lanterns, borne aloft by the men with the spades, they made their somewhat gruesome way into the cemetery grounds. Henry shivered faintly as he glanced around him. The flickering lights cast ghostly shadows all about, and the headstones of the graves stretched away into the dismal distance like rows of grim and ghastly spectres.

"Here we are," said the cemetery official in business-like tones. "I think that this is the place you want, gentlemen. Wilkinson is the name, isn't it?"

Shelley nodded, and examined the headstone above the grave at which they had halted.

"That's it," he said briefly. "Carry on."

But before they had had time to start, another man approached.

"Sorry I'm late, Shelley," he said as he drew near. "Couldn't get here earlier. Had a troublesome case to get through. I rushed it as well as I could, but it just couldn't be done any sooner."

"I was wondering where you were, old man," Shelley murmured. "Still, you're in good time. This is Dr. Maguire, gentlemen," he explained. "Dr. Maguire is a pathologist, and will shortly be making a post-mortem examination of the late Professor Wilkinson. I thought it well that he should be here to make a more or less cursory examination of the body on its first exhumation, in case there were any symptoms obvious which would disappear in the time which must elapse before the full post-mortem is to be made."

Now the two men with spades set to with a will, first removing the turf from over the grave, then digging down into the rich brown earth beneath. They had placed their lanterns on the ground, and the flickering light from these was now more ghastly than ever. Shining unsteadily upward in the gloom, the little slice of unsteady light made the surrounding darkness seem blacker than before.

Henry found himself peering myopically into the distance, vainly trying to pierce the veil of dreary gloom that shut them in, that made this little group of men almost a world on their own, cut off from the warm friendliness of the outside universe. Again he shuddered as he heard the sudden rattle of one of the spades against a large stone in the ground. He stood on his toes and peered over the shoulder of the Home Office official at the two men who were still digging steadily on.

There was still, however, nothing to be seen. The earth came steadily up, spadeful by spadeful, and there was now a considerable heap accumulated beside the open grave. And still the men dug on. And still Henry peered at the diggers, wondering if in their minds there was any trace of nausea at the gruesome task which was theirs to perform. He supposed not. Presumably grave-diggers grew accustomed to their unpleasant association with man's mortality. For a moment Henry tried to picture himself as a grave-digger, but his imagination boggled at the task.

Then there came a sharp hiss of indrawn breath from Shelley. The Scotland Yard man, outwardly calm, was filled with excitement. This might well be the final link in a chain of unmistakable evidence—a chain leading to the scaffold.

His suppressed whistle was the first sign that the men had reached the coffin. Soon they were lifting the great oak box to the surface, where they gently laid it on the grass beside the open grave. Now…now…Henry told himself that he was on the point of unthinkable revelations. But when it came to the crucial moment of unscrewing and removing the lid he found himself unable to look. He looked away into the dimness of the distance, and listened to the remarks of the others.

"Well, doctor?" he heard Shelley ask.

The doctor murmured something, the exact meaning of which Henry did not catch, and then he said: "Looks quite normal to me, I must say, Shelley. Certainly no arsenic or anything like that, though I imagine that you weren't really expecting anything of that kind."

Shelley laughed gently. "As a matter of fact, doctor, I wasn't. I suppose, though, that you won't be able to say anything until after the p.-m."

"No." The doctor was quite emphatic on that point. "It looks an unpleasant sort of job, and it will probably be a pretty long one. Shall we say about midday tomorrow? After all, you've got your man under lock and key, haven't you?"

"Ye-es." Shelley did not seem to be any too certain. "I certainly hope so. And in any case, if this is to be, as you say, a longish job, there's no point in my trying to hurry you over it. The only result of that would be to make you miss something important—and in a murder case we can't afford to run any risk of that."

So back they went to Scotland Yard, where Shelley shook Henry warmly by the hand, and bade him a cheerful "Good night."

"What about the result of the post-mortem?" asked Henry anxiously.

"What about it?" returned Shelley.

"Am I to be told what happens?"

"I am making no rash promises," answered Shelley with a smile. "Still, if you call around sometime tomorrow afternoon, I will do my best to satisfy your curiosity, Mr. Fairhurst. I have little doubt of what the result will be. But we shall see."

And with that Henry had to be content, though he felt that the complete absence of results made a strange anti-climax to an evening of the most outrageous excitement. But there was an even deeper depth of anti-climax to be reached, for when he reached Streatham again he had to concoct a purely fictitious account of his evening's employment to satisfy his sister's questionings. And Sarah had an awkward habit of asking almost unanswerable questions, and of sniffing unbelievingly when a reasonably good lie was concocted on the spur of the moment in reply to them.

Shelley was excited the next day when Dr. Maguire came around to Scotland Yard to report on the post-mortem examination of Professor Wilkinson.

"Well?" asked the detective as soon as the doctor entered the room. "What's the news, man?"

The doctor slowly and methodically removed his gloves and placed them on the table. Then he divested himself of his coat and folded it carefully, his deliberation almost driving Shelley insane.

"Not good news, I fear," he said at length.

"What do you mean? Was he murdered? What was the poison?" It was not often that Shelley lost control of himself to this extent, but he had counted much on this exhumation, and he hoped that the evidence would be enough to make a conviction a fairly easy matter.

"Professor Wilkinson," said Dr. Maguire slowly, choosing his words with care, "was suffering from long-established valvular disease of the heart. He died, quite simply, from heart failure. There was no evidence of any poison in the body at all."

"He was not murdered?"

"He was not murdered."

"He died a perfectly natural death?"

"He died a perfectly natural death."

Shelley picked up a pencil that lay on the desk before him and toyed with it idly. His heart sank within him. Had he been building up his whole case on a false theory? Had he committed the unforgivable sin of making his theory before he had enough facts on which to build? Who could tell? At any rate, there was no doubt that he would have to think the whole affair out again from the beginning. There was no doubt at all about that.

"Are you dead certain about that, doctor?" he asked, hoping against hope that there might be somewhere a loophole which would let him through.

"Dead certain," answered the doctor.

"Then what do we do next?"

"That," said the doctor, "is a matter for you to decide."

And as he left the room he saw Shelley lean his elbows on the desk, his chin propped on his clenched fists, his brow deeply furrowed with thought. Poor old Shelley, he thought. What a muddle! Where would it all lead?

Chapter XII

The Will Again

Mr. Fairhurst shook his head despondently.

"I'm afraid, my dear Miss Arnell, that there is little to be done," he said.

Violet Arnell gazed mournfully at him, tears forming in her eyes.

"Now, don't be silly, Henry," snapped his sister. "If all you can do is be a Job's comforter like that, then you're a bigger fool than I took you for, and that's a pity."

"Well," Henry argued, "if all that the police will tell me is that Wilkinson died a natural death, that Mr. Baker was on the spot (that is, at Pinner) at which he could easily have put a poisoned sweet in the packet in your father's pocket, and that he was undoubtedly outside the British Museum gates (if not inside them) on the night when Crocker was murdered, what can I do?"

"Do something, Henry," snapped Sarah. She was clearly on tenterhooks, disliking the idea of seeing Violet Arnell in such a tearful, woebegone state.

"There's only one thing," Henry added, after considerable deep thought, "that occurs to me."

"And that is…?" Violet Arnell awaited his words with an eagerness which was exceedingly flattering to his vanity.

"That is—your father's will," he announced, and then looked at her to see what effect this would have.

"But what use do you think that can be?" she asked in plaintive tones.

Henry did his best to look impressive. "I don't quite know," he said slowly. "The point is, in a case like this, where all the clues more or less peter out, to investigate as fully as we can the few clues that we have."

"But in what way is my father's will a clue?"

"I don't know," said Henry again. "But it is one of the few things which we have, and we must do our best to see what we can make of it."

Violet Arnell smiled. It was not a very triumphant smile—it was, as a matter of fact, a very milk-and-watery smile, but the fact of its managing to break through the hitherto uniform gloom of her countenance was something to be grateful for, and Henry felt quite a hero in consequence. He was, however, quite prepared to admit that the smile was due more to her imagination than to any prowess which he had yet achieved as a detective.

"As a matter of fact," she said, "I have it here in my handbag. I have been carrying it around with me, as Inspector Shelley, after photographing it, told me to take great care of it, as it might be an important clue later on."

Henry beamed. "There; what did I tell you?" he said. "An important clue. And I went straight for it, you see."

"You might," said Sarah with a supercilious sniff, "do something more than talk about it, Henry. Then we might think a little more of you as a detective."

Violet produced the document from her handbag, and handed it to Henry. He read it aloud.

"This is the last will and testament of me, Julius Arnell, Professor Emeritus in the University of Portavon. I hereby give and bequeath all my property to my daughter, Violet Arnell, for her sole use during her lifetime. At her death it is to go, whether she has issue or not, to my nephew, Moses Moss, to belong to him and his heirs and assigns, absolutely."

Henry looked up. "Is that the sort of will that you would have expected your father to make?" he asked.

"Yes," she answered.

"Written in blue ink," murmured Henry, "and dated December 3, 1936."

"What's that?" Violet Arnell looked at him in surprise.

"Written in blue ink, I said," Henry repeated, "and dated December 3, 1936."

An air of puzzled bewilderment came over her face. She frowned and gazed hard at the document, her eyes puckering up in surprise.

"But…but…I don't understand," she said.

"What don't you understand?" asked Henry patiently.

"My father always wrote everything in blue ink in the past," she said. "It was a little fad of his. But there was some trouble about a book that he wrote in the summer of 1936. The girl who typed it out from his written manuscript said that his bright blue ink—just this colour, you know—was trying to her eyes." She paused.

"Go on," said Henry.

"In the autumn of 1936, my father told me to throw away the blue ink, and get in a supply of the more usual blue-black. You know, the stuff that goes black when it's been dry for a few hours."

"I know." Henry was all excitement now. This was the real thing, he told himself. At last it began to look as if they were on the track of something big!

"And at the time that the will was written *there was no blue ink in the house!*"

They looked at each other in silence. Sarah sniffed, and said: "Well; what are you going to do about it? Some fishy work going on there, I'll be bound."

"I don't quite understand it," Henry admitted frankly. "It just doesn't seem to make sense. Why, if your father had no blue ink, did he go to the trouble of making his will in ink of that colour?"

"But…but…d-d-don't you see?" Violet Arnell stammered in her excitement.

"I'm afraid I don't. It's a very remarkable business, but I can't see what it means," said Henry, a puzzled frown creasing his forehead.

"It means," said Violet in impressive tones, "that my father did *not* write that will."

"Oh, come, come, Miss Arnell," Henry protested. "I don't think that you can exactly say that. After all, what grounds have you for saying—"

Violet interrupted him. "My father," she said again, "did *not* write that will."

"Mightn't there be a fountain-pen knocking about somewhere with some of the blue ink left in it?" was Henry's next suggestion. "After all, it was only a few months from the time that the blue ink was thrown away. And there might easily be some left in a fountain-pen."

"My father never used a fountain-pen," she explained. "He was a very old-fashioned man in some ways, and he had a rooted objection to fountain-pens—said they made everyone write alike. He used an old steel-nibbed pen. And, although I have a fountain-pen, I never used the blue ink. I disliked the colour."

"Well, it is, of course, possible," said Henry. "And now, Miss Arnell, we may as well investigate this will a little further. I presume that Inspector Shelley has tested it for finger-prints?"

"Yes."

"Any found?"

"No."

"Well, let's have a look at the paper." Henry held it up to the light, and made a note on a pad that was before him.

"1937 Bond. Barnes and Co., Chiswick," he said. "That doesn't tell us very much, does it? Might be worth enquiring of them if they could identify it, but it really doesn't seem likely."

"Wait a minute. Wait a minute." Violet Arnell was getting excited once more.

"What's worrying you now?" Henry grunted out the question. This business of detection, he told himself, was not all milk and honey, by any means.

"1937 Bond," she said quietly.

"What about that?"

"The will is dated 1936, remember."

"Oh, that's nothing." Henry waved away the suggestion with an airy wave of his hand "Those figures don't mean anything. My note-paper is called '1718 Bond,' but that doesn't mean that it was made in the year 1718, or anywhere near it. Probably the figure is just a trade-mark, and that's all there is to it."

"I'm not so sure. I think it's worth finding out, anyhow," Violet Arnell objected.

Henry sighed. "Very well," he agreed. "I suppose that there's no harm in ringing them up, and just asking them about it."

He drew the telephone towards him, dialled a number, and then waited.

"That Barnes and Co.?" he asked. "I wonder if you can tell me at what date you commenced putting your '1937

Bond' paper on the market? When? Oh, yes, that settles my problem very well, thank you. Thank you very much. Good-bye."

He turned to face the others, and his complexion was the colour of milk.

"Your idea was right, Miss Arnell," he said quietly.

"It is a forgery," she announced.

"Quite right. It is a forgery. That paper was originally intended to be called 'Coronation Bond,' in celebration of the coronation of King George VI, but another firm took the name first. They therefore decided to call it '1937 Bond.'"

"And when was it first put on the market?" she asked.

"On February 10, 1937, two months after the will was supposed to have been written!"

"Again, Mr. Fairhurst?" Shelley almost laughed as the little man twisted awkwardly in the chair at Scotland Yard.

"Again, Inspector." Henry found the subject very difficult to broach.

"Well, what's the meaning of this visit?"

"I have found something very important, sir. Something which may alter the whole complexion of this case."

"Still think young Baker is not guilty?"

"I don't know what bearing this has on his guilt, but it is something that I think you should know. After that, you can do what you like about it."

"Well, carry on," announced Shelley cheerfully.

"The will of the late Professor Arnell is a forgery," announced Henry in his grimmest tones.

"Sure?" Shelley snapped out the monosyllable.

"Certain." And Henry told briefly of their investigations of an hour or two before. Then he had a revelation of the astounding efficiency of Scotland Yard.

"Where did you leave Miss Arnell?" Shelley asked.

"She went home to Pinner, and I said I would ring her up when you had told me what you thought about this business of the forgery."

"What's her number?"

Henry told him, and Shelley drew the telephone towards him, and rapidly got through to the number required. After holding the receiver for a few minutes, obviously listening to the ringing at the other end, he quietly replaced it on its hook, and picked up another 'phone.

"Send me Sergeant Cunningham, a flying-squad car, and half a dozen plain-clothes men," he said.

"I don't understand, Inspector," Henry objected.

"You'll understand soon enough," snapped Shelley. "No time to waste."

Now Cunningham entered, and Shelley, in sharp, staccato tones, gave him his orders.

"You remember Miss Arnell's house at Pinner?" he said.

Cunningham nodded.

"Well, somewhere between there and Streatham," his chief told him, "I think Miss Arnell has disappeared. See if you can get on her trail."

"Disappeared?" Cunningham looked completely amazed.

Shelley looked at Henry again.

"Did she go by bus?" he asked.

Henry nodded. In this atmosphere of brisk efficiency it seemed unnecessary to say anything. And in any case Shelley had said that it was urgent, and he did not want to waste time.

"Follow the bus routes, and see if you can find any account of a young lady resembling Miss Arnell being picked up by a car," Shelley went on. "If you can't trace her any other way, see if you can find a bus leaving Streatham at—what time would it be, Mr. Fairhurst?"

"Eight o'clock," murmured Henry, completely mystified by all this bustle, and not understanding this turn of events at all.

"Eight o'clock. Right. Got that, Cunningham?" asked Shelley.

"Yes, sir," Cunningham answered dutifully.

"Take the car I've ordered, and the half-dozen men. And hurry. She's in real danger. I'll never forgive myself if…if…" He paused, and Cunningham rapidly left the room.

"What do you think has happened to her, Inspector?" asked Henry.

"I don't know. Wish I did," answered Shelley. "It's the vague things like this that cause the trouble."

Now he picked up the 'phone again, and spoke rapidly.

"See if you can spot any traces of forgery in that photostat of the will of Professor Arnell, Mac," he said. "There are some documents by the man in the file in Room 126. I'm pretty sure it's a forgery, but it's as well to get confirmatory evidence, if I can."

"But what," asked Henry, when the detective had replaced the telephone receiver on its hook once more, "is the meaning of it, Mr. Shelley?"

"There can be only one meaning of that will being forged, my dear sir," answered Shelley. "You recall that it left the money to Miss Arnell. Well, it is just possible that Mr. Baker forged it. Though I don't think, if he did, he'd be so foolish as to leave the money to her for life only. No."

"Then who did?"

"That's what I'd like to know."

"Why did you think that Miss Arnell would be likely to have disappeared?" asked Henry.

"Because she is a very rich woman. And because her death means that Mr. Moses Moss has a lot of money. That's why!"

"And you think that Moses Moss is the murderer?"

"It looks very much like it," Shelley admitted.

Suddenly Henry gazed at Shelley in horror. A chill ran down his spine, and his very blood ran cold in his veins.

"But that means, Inspector," he said, "that means that there is a possibility that Moses Moss has got hold of Miss Arnell. That means that he may have kidnapped her, and taken her away somewhere."

Shelley nodded glumly. "It not only means that, my dear Mr. Fairhurst," he said quietly. "It means that Mr. Moses Moss may well be contemplating another murder."

Chapter XIII

Cunningham on the Trail

Cunningham leaned forward eagerly in his seat at the back of the flying-squad car, peering over the driver's shoulder at the streaming road ahead. Rain had started, and the streets were muddy mirrors in which the headlamps of passing cars reflected brilliantly.

Soon they were outside Henry Fairhurst's house at Streatham, and here the trail really began.

"I wonder," mused Cunningham, "if there is any through route from here to Pinner? Are there any buses which run through, do you think?"

"Yes, Sergeant," said one of his companions. "I used to go with a girl out this way, and so I know."

"Splendid," said Cunningham. "Which way?"

"Out on the main road," said the other. "First on the right and then second on the left. The buses start out there—it's the main road, you see."

"First right, second left," snapped Cunningham, and the driver obeyed promptly.

"Now what?" asked Cunningham as they got there.

"Here's the bus," remarked the constable as a great red giant came lumbering down the street towards them. "If we follow that, I reckon we shall be following the way that the young lady went. Yes—see, it's South Harrow and Pinner that it goes to."

Cunningham chafed at the inactivity now forced upon him. Their car, with its great potentialities of speed, crawled along in the wake of the great bus, stopped when the London Transport vehicle stopped, and started again when the passengers had alighted and made their slippery way to the pavement.

The rain was descending in sheets, and along the lengthy road ahead of them the yellow glow of the street lamps stretched in a seemingly endless line into the distance. The paler colour of gas lamps took their place, and then the hideous sheen of the newer type of daylight lamps made their faces look ghastly as they peered at the road where it slipped away, an endless shiny ribbon ahead.

After this had continued for some time they saw a traffic policeman, a solemn, solitary figure in a streaming mackintosh cape, standing in the middle of the road where another important artery of traffic crossed it at right angles. Cunningham spoke excitedly.

"Stop!" he said. "Let's see if this fellow has anything to say."

They stopped, and Cunningham pulled down the window at his side of the car, and popped his head out, looking intently at the policeman.

"Here," he said, and the constable approached. Cunningham showed him his authorisation as a Scotland Yard man, and described what they were after.

"A young lady," he said, "was travelling on a bus to Pinner and Harrow. She was probably hailed by a young man"—and he described Moses Moss—"who took her off the bus, probably in his car."

Stolidly the constable shook his head. "Sorry," he said. "Seen nothing like that, Sergeant. Nothing at all out of the usual has happened here this evening, I'm afraid. Sorry I can't help you."

Cunningham shut the window with a slam, and ordered the driver to go on. The madcap chase after nothingness started once more. He remembered similar chases in the past, when he had been in the company of Shelley, thought of the times that he had spent in racing thus after desperate characters, never quite knowing what might be waiting for him at his journey's end. Never before, however, had he chased something as vague as this, never before had he been engaged in trying to track down something that might never exist at all. Still, it was enough for him that Shelley had a "hunch" on the matter, for he was quite prepared to back Shelley's "hunches" as much as he would back another man's certainties.

Soon they found another traffic policeman, but here again they drew blank, and, his temper fast deteriorating, Cunningham ordered the policeman at the wheel to drive on once more. And again this happened…and again…and again. At last Cunningham began to think that the whole affair was the craziest of wild-goose chases, for they were now drawing near to Pinner. Above them on the hill they could see the tower of Harrow Church, and still they had not succeeded in finding the least trace of Miss Arnell and her possibly hypothetical kidnapper.

At last, however, just as they emerged on to the main street of Pinner, still "old-world," if in a somewhat more self-conscious manner than of yore, they struck oil. They found a policeman who seemed to have some memory of Miss Arnell and a man who took her off the bus.

"Yes," he said. "I remember a fellow taking a girl off a bus. Just along the main street here, it was, just by the bus-stop down there. She was a pretty girl"—here Cunningham swiftly produced a portrait of Violet Arnell with which he had been careful to provide himself, and it was rapidly identified by the constable.

"What happened to her?" Cunningham asked with some eagerness.

"She was on the bus, as I said, and a young fellow came along in a low racing car—one of them noisy things that makes a roar as they go along," said the constable. "He stopped the car just in front of the bus, and jumped out. He hopped on to the bus, and must have spoken to her, for she got off the bus with him."

"Did she seem to know him?"

"Now you mention it, I shouldn't have said she did."

"Why not?" Cunningham was more eager than ever now. It began to look as if he was getting on to the trail with a vengeance. He had scarcely dared to hope that he would do so, his successive failures on the long road having driven a rod of pessimism into his soul.

"Well." The policeman scratched his head thoughtfully. "'Tis difficult to lay my tongue on any exact reason. But I think it looked as if she was arguing with him, saying 'What the devil do you want with me?'—if you understand what I mean."

"I think I do," said Cunningham, and prepared to play his trump card. He fished in his pocket and produced a photograph of Moses Moss.

"Was this the man?" he asked.

Again the slow policeman scratched his head.

"It might be," he said cautiously.

"What do you mean, it might be?" asked Cunningham in irritated tones.

"I mean what I say, Sergeant," responded the other. "It's not easy to identify anybody in the light of these lamps when they're nigh on fifty feet away."

"Still, you identified the lady without any difficulty," Cunningham objected.

"Ah, but that's different. You see," he said with what was almost a leer, "young ladies don't grow beards."

"Beards?" Cunningham was almost startled by this new item of information.

"Yes. The young fellow had a beard. One of them little black things, like a tuft of grass stuck on the end of their chins," explained the constable.

"Black?"

"Yes."

Cunningham rapidly sketched in a neat little beard on the photograph, and handed it to the policeman again.

"What about it now?" he asked. "Would you say that it looked like him now?"

"No," said the man decisively. "You've drawn the beard a bit more pointed than his was, but I'm dead sure that it wasn't the fellow. His head was a different shape. 'Twas more squarer, if you follow what I mean."

"H'm." Cunningham was nonplussed. This was a real problem. If the kidnapper was not Moses Moss, who could it be? It was, of course, possible that the man was mistaken. Moss might have disguised himself effectively, and the disguise might even have seemed better than it was, so that the constable had been completely deceived by it. Still, on the other hand, it was possible that the young man who had taken Violet Arnell off the bus had not been Moses Moss at all, in which case they would have to begin their theorising all over again. Anyhow, that was Shelley's job, Cunningham reminded himself. His own immediate task was to get as much information as he could on the spot.

"What happened afterwards?" he asked.

"She got in his car and they drove off," answered the man.

"What direction?"

"They seemed to be making north," answered the other with a knowing smile. "Making for the Great North Road they were. Gretna Green, if you ask me."

"I didn't ask you," Cunningham snapped.

"Anything more, then?"

Cunningham pondered the matter for a while, wondering what Shelley would want to know about the case, when he came to hand in his report later.

"One thing," he said at length. "Do you happen to know who were conductor and driver on the bus?"

"As it happens, I do," answered the policeman. "In my place, you see, we get to know most of the regular men on the routes passing here."

"Who were they?"

"The driver was Harry Davison, and the conductor Bill Angelus," answered the policeman. All his replies, Cunningham noticed, were given without any hesitation. He was clearly a man who used his eyes. Even though he might occasionally be irritatingly obtuse, he had nevertheless that gift of acute observation which is of such vital importance to the first-rate policeman.

"What depot would they clock in at?" asked the man from Scotland Yard.

"Willesden, I think," replied the other.

"Which way?" asked Cunningham.

"Straight through here," answered his informant. "You can't miss it. Just follow straight through along the main road. You'll be there in a quarter of an hour or twenty minutes at the most."

This time Cunningham did not chafe at his inactivity. The fast car was full out. Such things as speed limits were forgotten, and they skidded perilously at one or two sharp corners. But they soon got to Willesden, and were, before very long, in earnest colloquy with the manager of the bus depot.

Cunningham explained that he wanted a word with Harry Davison and Bill Angelus, adding that a suspicious character was rumoured to have been on the bus which was in their charge that afternoon and evening.

The manager glanced at the clock. "They'll be in any moment now," he said. "As a matter of fact, they're two or three minutes overdue already, but it's difficult to keep up to time schedules with this beastly weather. The roads get so slippery that they have to be mighty careful with those heavy buses."

Soon the two men arrived. Harry Davison was a heavy-jowled man with grizzled grey hair, and Bill Angelus a small man with bright red hair.

Cunningham explained his mission, and the driver announced at once that he knew nothing whatever about the incident, which, of course, was what the detective had anticipated, for it was not to be expected that the man in the front seat of the bus should have seen anything that was happening behind him. He would be far too intent in watching the road ahead and on listening for the conductor's bell, signalling the restart.

"I remember it, mister," said the conductor, and Cunningham breathed again. The information had taken some tracking down, but it looked as if he was to get the required confirmation of the evidence already gained in Pinner.

"Yes," he said. "What happened? Tell me the whole story from the beginning."

Bill took a deep breath and started.

"She got on in Streatham," he said, "and took a sixpenny ticket to Pinner."

"Do you usually remember each one of your passengers like this, Bill?" asked Cunningham, and the little man grinned cheerfully.

"Not everyone, by any means, governor," he said. "But I do remember anybody when there's anything peculiar happened to 'em, like there did to this young lady, as I'm about to tell you."

"I see. Carry on."

"Well, she sat there, reading her paper, and then, when we stopped at the first stop in Pinner High Street there was a big racing car roared up and stopped just ahead of us—I think Harry must have seen it, didn't you?" he added, turning to the driver, who nodded surly confirmation.

"The young fellow who drove this car hopped out quick, as soon as he was stopped in front of us. He came around to the bus, jumped in, and went straight up to the young lady. 'Miss Arnell, I think,' he says, in a thick, foreign-sounding sort of voice."

"Foreign-sounding?" said Cunningham. "What do you mean? Had he a foreign accent?"

"Not exactly accent. More like a thick, deep, rough sort of voice. Sort of German voice, if you know what I mean," added the conductor, obviously finding it difficult to make his exact meaning clear.

"Yes, I think I understand," said Cunningham. "And what did the lady say?"

"She said 'Who are you?' in a frightened sort of voice. And he said 'I'm your friend. H.B. is in trouble, and he sent me to you.'"

Cunningham was fairly jumping with excitement now.

"What happened next?" he asked.

"She said 'Has he escaped?' and the man said 'We can't talk here. If you'll come with me I'll take you straight to him.' And he took hold of her wrist and fairly dragged her off the bus. As we started off I glanced back and saw them getting into his car. So I reckon that he was right. He was taking her off to see some pal of hers. Maybe her boy-friend had escaped from the jug or something," the conductor added helpfully.

"What was the man like?" asked Cunningham.

"Weedy little chap," said the conductor. "About five foot five, I should think. Thin and miserable-looking. He had black hair, long, greasy-looking, and untidy, and he had a little black beard—a silly little beard like a lot of the fellows calling themselves artists what we sometimes pick up out Chelsea way."

"That's very helpful, Bill," announced Cunningham. "I'm very much obliged to you."

He produced his photograph of Moses Moss, on which the beard was still pencilled. "This the fellow?" he asked.

Bill shook his head.

"The beard may be the wrong shape," Cunningham warned him. "I think that it may be a disguise, and I have to draw it in on a photograph of the man when he was clean-shaved."

"No," said Bill firmly. "That's not the fellow. He had a different shape face from that photo. Ask Harry here."

"This the man, Harry?" asked Cunningham, and Harry looked doubtful.

"Well," he said, "I really didn't get a very good view of him, and I wouldn't swear to it. It might well be him, for all I could tell."

"And that," said Cunningham, as he sped back to Shelley to give an account of his evening's work, "is about as unsatisfactory a piece of identification as I could imagine."

Chapter XIV

The Case Against Moses Moss

Cunningham grinned. He had given Shelley a full account of his investigations in the wild hinterlands of Streatham and Pinner, and Shelley had expressed his very real pleasure and satisfaction that the sergeant had been enabled to get so far in such short time.

"Mind you, Cunningham," he added in warning tones, "I don't say that we've really got anywhere yet; it's much too soon to start theorising. Still, I think that we can congratulate ourselves on having got past a very tasty red herring without wasting much time."

"Red herring?" Cunningham was not always able to follow the workings of his chief's somewhat nimbler mind, and on these occasions he was compelled simply to wait for the explanation which he knew would shortly be forthcoming from Shelley.

"Yes," smiled his chief. "Red herring, I said, and red herring I meant—i.e., namely, and to wit, Mr. Baker."

"Baker's innocent, of course."

"Of course. As pretty a piece of framing-up as I've ever

encountered. And, by Jove," added Shelley, "we very nearly fell for it."

He rang the bell on his desk, and the waiting constable from outside the door came in.

"Message for all stations," said Shelley, and the constable's note-book and pencil were produced as if by magic.

"Pull in at once, man with black beard and black greasy hair," Shelley dictated. "He is in a racing car, believed to be making north, and is accompanied by a young lady…" And he went on to give a detailed description of Violet Arnell. "Add that photograph of the young lady will be following," he said, "and add that the man may be armed and is certainly a dangerous character—probably a murderer. He has killed twice and may kill again."

"That all, sir?" murmured the constable in almost bored tones, treating this sensational matter as merely part of the everyday routine—as indeed it was to him, being nothing more unusual than a business letter to a typist in an office.

"Ye-es," said Shelley thoughtfully. "I don't think I've missed anything essential—or how does it strike you, Sergeant?"

"Strikes me as being perfectly all right, sir," said Cunningham.

"Good. Then get that on the wires to all stations," snapped Shelley briskly. "And tell them to send first to all stations north of London—up as far as Manchester and Sheffield, say. I shouldn't think they could have got much further than that, although they have managed to get several hours' lead on us."

The constable left, and Shelley smiled grimly. "Well, we now sit and wait for news, Cunningham," he said. "If I were you I should go home and try to snatch a few hours' sleep. We may well have an exciting piece of chasing ahead of us tomorrow."

"You think so, sir?"

"I hope so."

"Hope?"

"Well." Shelley looked serious. "If we don't get some news within a few hours, I'm afraid we shan't get any," he said.

"Whatever do you mean, sir?"

"Don't forget that Moss is a murderer."

"And you think he'll murder Miss Arnell?"

"I don't think he'd hesitate for a moment. I can't understand why he didn't kill her in London as soon as he had managed to get her into that car of his—he may even have done so, though somehow I think not."

"But what do you think has happened, sir?"

"You really mean that you'd like to hear me talking about this confounded case, O my Cunningham?"

Cunningham grinned. "Yes," he said.

"Then it shall be on your own head," said Shelley. "I will tell you what I think has happened. You know my weakness for arguing the whole thing out like this, and, anyhow, I want you to have all the facts before you. You don't know what I've been doing in the time while you were dashing about the respectable suburbs."

"Carry on, sir," said Cunningham, and Shelley willingly complied.

"I think that the will was a forgery. Moss was in a desperate position—for a reason which I will tell you presently and which I have only discovered quite recently—and he saw that the only way of putting things right was to get old Professor Arnell's money left to him. But he scarcely knew Professor Arnell—he had merely heard him referred to as his rich uncle. How was he to ensure it?"

"How?" murmured Cunningham.

"He could forge a will. But a will needed to have two witnesses. Then there came the chance of Dr. Wilkinson's death at the British Museum. Moss had seen Wilkinson as one of Arnell's friends, and there was one witness ready made."

"It doesn't matter, then," said Cunningham, "if a witness to a will dies before the testator."

"Not a bit," said Shelley. "If that made a will invalid half the wills in the country would be wrong."

"I see."

"Well," said Shelley, "that disposes of one witness. The other witness—Crocker—very nearly muddled the whole affair for Moss. I looked through the files of *The Times* today, and I found that Crocker's death was wrongly reported a few weeks ago. There was an error. Another man of the same name, also living in Oxford, had died, and it was reported as being the man whose murder we so nearly witnessed."

"I suppose Moss found out his mistake only just in time?" Cunningham suggested.

"Yes. So Crocker had to die. But Moss had already tried to inveigle Miss Arnell's young man in the case, and he saw in Crocker's death the ideal opportunity of killing two birds with one stone. So he wrote that note, bringing young Baker up to town, and made sure that he would be in the vicinity of the murder. I have no doubt that he inveigled his victim to the neighbourhood of the British Museum by some similar means. It all sounds very complicated when I describe it to you like this, but it's quite simple really."

"And why make the will to benefit Miss Arnell and him-self after her death?" asked Cunningham.

"It does seem rather curious, I must admit," said Shelley. "Still, the main point would be to distract the immediate suspicions as to himself, which would naturally arise if the Professor had left the money to an almost unknown cousin, and had disinherited his only daughter."

"H'm." Cunningham did not seem to be altogether con-vinced by this explanation.

"And I have a vague suspicion that Moss hoped to marry the young lady himself, when her fiancé had been hanged for the murder of her father." Shelley paused to see what would be the effect of this revelation upon his colleague.

Cunningham seemed to take this as probable, and agreed that it appeared to be quite a likely attitude for the murderer to take up.

"I think, though," he added, "that you said something about new facts."

"Oh, yes." Shelley recalled himself to the present. "This evening, while you were getting hold of those useful facts about the kidnapping of Miss Arnell, I made some enquiries as to Moss's financial status."

"Yes?"

"Yes. And he was practically bankrupt. Up to the eyes in debt, didn't know where to turn for cash. So that explains a whole lot more, gives him an adequate motive, and shows that he wanted to get out of the hands of the money-lenders who had a pretty tight grip on him."

"Money-lenders?"

"Yes. Remember Victor Isaacs, the moneylender of Ludgate Hill?"

"Can't say I do."

"Maybe you haven't met him professionally. Nasty piece of work. Greasy little fellow, who will do anything for a few pounds. He's one of those unpleasant people whom the Fascists are so fond of portraying as the typical Jew. Nothing of the sort really, of course, and to call him such is a libel on the Jewish race."

"And Moss owed him money?"

"Yes; to the tune of several thousands. I went around to Isaacs's office, and, though Isaacs himself wasn't on duty—only turns up for an hour or two a day, I imagine—I managed to scare his assistant into giving me full details of the transactions in which Mr. Moss was concerned. They didn't have any indication of the security offered, which is itself pretty suspicious. But there was no doubt at all that Moss owed him a pile—and he was pressing for, at any rate, a partial settlement. And there's the motive!"

"But who do you think actually did the kidnapping?" Cunningham objected.

"Moss himself," answered Shelley promptly.

"In disguise?"

"Naturally."

"That's possible, but we shall have the very devil of a job to prove it," said Cunningham.

"Think so? Why?"

"Well," said Cunningham with a sheepish grin, "you can't say that those busmen were precisely ideal witnesses to identify Moss, can you?"

"No. But identification should be easy enough when we get him with Miss Arnell a prisoner in the north of England somewhere—for I imagine that's where they're making for. A criminal always makes for the part of the country that he knows best. When he's on the run he thinks that he has a better chance of avoiding the police there."

"Moss knows the north of England?"

"Yes. He lived in Leeds for several years, and I think that it's in Leeds that we shall catch him."

"Well, I hope so," said Cunningham, and then another thought struck him.

"Wilkinson was not murdered at all, then?" he asked.

"Oh, no. I should have mentioned that. The autopsy on Wilkinson, as you know, showed that no poison was present. He died of heart failure, and had suffered from valvular disease of the heart for many years. It was merely coincidence that he had died at the British Museum. It is possible, indeed, that this was what gave Moss the idea of his plot."

"I see," said Cunningham. "And what do we do next?"

"As I said, wait for the results to come in. There's nothing else that we can do, really. Every policeman in Great Britain will be looking for them by now, and within the next few hours we shall know something about it."

The telephone rang, and Shelley eagerly grasped the receiver.

"What's that?" he said excitedly. "Put them through to here at once. This sounds important."

He waited for a moment and then spoke again. "Where?" Cunningham heard him ask. "Outskirts of Sheffield? Yes. On the main Manchester road? Yes. What time? Right. Your men chasing them? Right. We'll follow straight away."

"Found them, sir?" asked Cunningham.

"Yes," said Shelley. "They were seen half an hour ago by a man on point duty in Sheffield. Apparently they were making for Manchester—out on the main Manchester road from Sheffield, anyway. Look up trains for Sheffield, Cunningham. It looks to me as if we are soon to be in at the death."

Feverishly Cunningham took up a time-table and began searching it.

"Mr. Moss, we have you!" Shelley exclaimed, giving way to the somewhat melodramatic vein which was occasionally to be detected in him.

Then a constable entered. "A gentleman to see you, sir," he announced. "He wants to speak to you about the Arnell case—or so he says."

"Who is he?" asked Shelley.

"Won't give a name, sir."

"Train in forty minutes from St. Pancras, sir!" said Cunningham.

"I can give the gentleman ten minutes," snapped Shelley. "I only hope it isn't that little fathead Henry Fairhurst again."

The constable retired, then came back and threw open the door. Shelley and Cunningham gazed at each other as if they doubted their sanity. Shelley's case had been so carefully constructed that neither of them doubted that it was accurate in every detail. The kidnapper of Miss Violet Arnell was now somewhere outside Sheffield, speeding along in a fast car, and closely pursued by the Yorkshire police. Yet… yet…their visitor was none other than *Mr. Moses Moss*!

Chapter XV

The Adventures of Violet Arnell

Violet had felt a considerable access of pleasure when she made her way from Henry Fairhurst's home out to the place where she was to catch a bus for home. It really seemed as if they were on the track of something, and as if her young man had some chance of getting free before long. All the way home she went over the situation in her mind. The whole matter seemed incredibly complicated, and she felt little doubt that Harry Baker had been "framed-up" by some unknown but implacable enemy. That she herself might be in any danger never occurred to her, and it was with considerable surprise that she greeted the strange-looking man with greasy black hair and a ragged black beard who accosted her in the bus as it drew up in Pinner High Street. He seemed quite a young man, and she was surprised at the apparent carelessness in his personal appearance.

"Miss Arnell, I think," he said in the guttural tones of one to whom English is a foreign language.

"Yes," said Violet. "Who are you?"

"I," he said in tones which seemed to suggest the urgency of complete secrecy, "am your friend. I want to tell you that our mutual friend Mr. H. B. is in trouble, and he has sent me to fetch you."

"Has he escaped?" asked Violet excitedly.

"I cannot answer any questions just yet," replied the man. "In any case, we can't talk here. If you'll just come a little way with me I can assure you that I'll lead you straight to him."

He suddenly grasped her wrist in fingers of iron, and, almost before she came to any realisation of what was happening, Violet found herself being led off the bus, and into the waiting car—a low, rakish model of the aggressive kind. Almost without opposition she let herself be led into it. It was possible, she told herself, that this was a trap, that there was really something curiously "fishy" about the whole affair, and yet she did not hesitate, for if Harry really was in trouble she could not hesitate. Her duty, after all, was to be by his side.

As soon as they had moved off, however, she felt qualms of distrust sweeping over her. The personality of the queer man by her side was not precisely such as to inspire her with much confidence, and she began to ask him questions.

"Has Harry escaped, and are we going to him?" she asked, but her companion shook his head grimly.

"I fear that I can answer no questions," he said. "My orders are to drive you to our destination without telling you anything about where we are going, or why."

"But that's just nonsense!" exclaimed Violet in angry tones. "You don't think that I am going wherever you like to take me, knowing nothing about it, do you? You don't think I am going to put myself utterly in your hands without some sort of indication of what is happening?"

He chuckled. His chuckle, too, was of a queer, eerie kind. It seemed to echo in the car as it rushed through the streets of London, the long rows of lamps streaming past.

"You *are* in my hands already, my dear young lady," he said with a grin. "Whether you like it or not, you are coming with me to where I am ordered to take you. That is final, my dear young lady, and I have nothing more to say about the matter."

"But I demand to know where I am being taken," Violet announced. "You have no right to take me away like this, no right whatever."

Again he chuckled, and again Violet felt a little shiver of apprehension run down her spine at the sound. It was as if he had announced some dreadful fate for her, a fate which he, in a perverted, insane manner, found infinitely amusing and promising in prospect.

"You may demand whatever you wish," he said in his strangely foreign accent. "But I do not guarantee that you will succeed in getting what you demand."

"But this is monstrous," Violet was beginning to say, but he interrupted her, turning towards her with teeth bared in a hideous, humourless grin.

"Will you please oblige me by keeping quiet?" he said fiercely. "If you will not do so I shall be obliged to take means to silence you."

"What do you mean?"

"I should think my meaning is clear enough."

"I'm afraid," said Violet, "that it is not."

"Well, then, if I must be explicit. If you do not keep quiet and cease to worry me by your foolish chatter, I shall be obliged to tie you up and gag you, so that there shall be no danger of your so distracting me that there will be a very serious accident."

"Oh!" Violet shrank back into her corner of the car, her head spinning at this revelation of the malignancy of her companion. Into what dreadful company had she stumbled? What on earth had happened to turn the man so bitterly against her? Or had he been her enemy from the start? Bravely she forced herself to the realisation that this was a trap, after all; that she was being whisked off to some unknown place for some unknown purpose; and that, though Harry Baker might well be freed when the information which she and Mr. Fairhurst had ferreted out was brought to the attention of the police, it seemed very unlikely that she would be there to welcome him on his release from prison.

She glanced out of the car as it sped along the streets. She could not, however, make out where they were. All London streets look pretty much alike at night, and there seemed no chance of identifying any particular one in passing through it. Her hope was that the car might be driven too fast. It certainly seemed as if they might well be exceeding the speed limit. If a policeman stopped the driver she felt that it might easily happen that she could utter some protest. And, surely, her captor (for as such she now thought of him) would not dare to stop her from speaking.

This did not happen. It seemed that he must have known precisely what he was doing, and carefully refrained from driving at more than thirty miles an hour in any built-up area.

Once they stopped at a crossing, where the traffic lights were against them, and she moved as if to get out. But her companion gripped her wrist in his fingers. He hissed into her ears: "Stay still!" Almost petrified with fright, she was unable to get free, and helplessly acquiesced in her continued imprisonment—for such, she decided, this really was.

On they sped, the night getting ever blacker, and the rain, which had caused Sergeant Cunningham such trouble in his attempt to find her, coming down in sheets. It struck the windscreen of the car as if with malice aforethought, but splashed off helplessly into the road.

By now they had left the last straggling houses of the outer suburbs of London behind, and were sweeping along a fine, broad road, where many cars passed them, and great lumbering lorries had to be passed in their turn.

"Is this the Great North Road?" she asked, and her companion nodded.

"It is," he said. "But I warn you: talk no more, or it will be the worse for you."

She subsided into silence. Clearly this man who had kidnapped her so fearlessly was absolutely without scruple. Obviously he was the murderer, she told herself, and her heart made a wild leap into her mouth at the thought.

At last, however, she thought of a way of leaving, at any rate, some sort of clue behind. It might never be picked up, but it did give her the satisfaction of knowing that she was doing her best to give the police—who would, she hoped, do their best to track this dreadful man to his lair, wherever that might be—some sort of chance of discovering her. So she cautiously opened her handbag, taking out her handkerchief and ostentatiously wiping her nose. Then she pretended to replace it in her bag, but really retained it in the palm of her hand, screwed into a little ball. As they swung around a corner in the road, she leaned towards the window, and gripped the little handle that opened it.

But her manœuvre had not passed unobserved. Again she felt the iron grip of the man's hand close around her wrist, and he muttered in her ear.

"Window's shut, I think."

"What do you mean?"

"This." He leaned across her, turned a little key which was in the door of the car, and then sank back in his seat. His eyes had been glued to the road ahead. He had not for a moment looked either at her or at the door, but she now found, when she tried to open the window of the car, that it was locked.

She could have cried with vexation. Her only chance of leaving some sort of clue behind her, some little thing (for her hand-kerchief, though tiny, was marked with her full name) which would enable Harry Baker or Mr. Fairhurst or the police, or all the three in collaboration, to get on her trail and rescue her before it was too late!

Now they swung into some big town. She gazed out of the window helplessly, trying to see where it could be, but was unable to catch any glimpse of a post office or anything else which would enable her to identify the town or city through which they were passing.

"Where are we?" she asked at length, but her companion merely shook his head, never uttering a word. Violet had never felt so helpless in her life. Where on earth could they be? What on earth could be the meaning of this wild dash through the night? It seemed the craziest thing, and yet, when she looked at the grim, determined face of her captor, the black beard on his chin waggling as he muttered to himself disjointed words in some uncouth Eastern tongue, she felt that he would not do anything unless it was in complete accord with some preconceived plan. It seemed utterly impossible that he would catch her and take her away like this unless there was some very real method in his madness, unless he had every intention of carrying out a plan matured to the last detail.

What could it be? She shrugged her shoulders hopelessly, and peered out into the darkness ahead. The rain had stopped now, but the roads still shone like sheets of polished glass in the vivid light of the car's headlamps. Not so many cars passed them now, though an occasional lorry rumbled past, its burly weight almost shaking the road as it rattled along.

Surely, she thought to herself, they could not be going for long like this. Then they came to another town, and this time she determined to make an effort to attract attention. Although they were going at a fair speed, she thought that it would not be too dangerous to throw herself out. She felt so desperate that anything would be better than to continue in this forced captivity, hurtling across England to an unknown fate in an unknown destination.

She gripped the handle of the car's door tightly, scarcely conscious that the car was coming to a standstill in a lonely street. As she managed to get the door open her captor, a rubber truncheon in his hand, hit her smartly across the back of the head. Violet did not know what had happened. She merely saw the flashes of vivid light which so often prelude violent unconsciousness, and then oblivion descended on her.

She came to in broad daylight. She was lying on a dirty bed in an untidy room. She sat up, but at once collapsed into a prone position again. Her head ached, and her every limb felt as if it had been passed through some machine which had mangled them terribly.

Gradually, however, she mastered her nausea, and sat up. She was in a small room, white-washed long ago, but now with walls of an indeterminate grey.

Besides the bed, the room contained merely a chair and a small occasional table. It was uncarpeted, and there was merely a small piece of oilcloth, of a grotesquely ugly pattern, beside the table, and was obviously meant for her to stand on when performing her toilette, for on the table there was resting a large jug of water and a basin, in which she splashed her face and hands, then feeling considerably better to face whatever might be coming her way.

She staggered to the window, which was barred on the outside, and then looked around. She was in the country, but what country she could not tell. Before her eyes was stretched a wide panorama of hill and vale. The hills were of an uneven brown colour, fading away into black in the distance, save where outcrops of cruel granite stuck grey fingers through the sparse, brown grass. A brown road stretched its ribbon length away into the distance, and immediately below her, outside the front door of the house, she supposed, was a low, racing car—presumably that which had brought her here from London.

There was only one grain of comfort to be extracted from the situation. She was still in England, for they would never have dared to take the car out of the country. The risk of shipping it would have been too great. Still, she might be almost anywhere. Certainly she had never seen anything like this bitter, grim landscape in her life before. It even exceeded in cruelty the Mendip Hills of her childhood and the Dartmoor village where she had once, in her schooldays, spent a holiday.

The door opened, and a man entered. It was the man who had captured her the night before. His hair was now brushed more or less tidily. His beard was a little more neatly trimmed. In fact, he looked almost civilised. But still the fire of enmity burned in his steady eyes.

"My dear Miss Arnell," he said in sarcastic tones, "I trust that we have made you comfortable in our humble way, and that you have no complaints to make as to our north-country hospitality?"

"I demand," replied Violet with some dignity, "to be released at once."

"Certainly," he said, smiling at her. "You shall be released very shortly; but there are a few little formalities which will, I fear, have to be complied with before that no doubt desirable consummation can be achieved. Our conditions are, I assure you, the merest formality; but I think that I shall have to give you a little rest before I go on to discuss them with you."

"Conditions?"

"That, my dear young lady, was the word that I have used."

"What are they?"

"That, as I said a moment ago, will have to wait until you are just the wee-est bit more able to discuss matters of business."

"Why do you say that?"

"Well," he explained, "you have gone through a somewhat difficult and trying experience; and I feel that I owe it to you to give you time to rest."

"I want no rest," snapped Violet. "I want to get out of here without delay. Tell me your conditions, and I will tell you if I can agree to them. I shouldn't be able to rest in this dreadful room, anyhow."

His eyebrows rose. "I see no reason for delay, my dear lady, if you do not," he said. "Let us talk business." He sat on the bed and faced her.

Chapter XVI

Revelations?

It took Shelley several seconds to recover from his astonishment when Moses Moss entered the room. They had decided that this man was the murderer, the kidnapper of Violet Arnell. And that kidnapper was quite certainly somewhere in the north of England at this very moment! But who could he be? Shelley racked his brains, but was totally unable to decide. However, it was obvious that the next move was to find out to what they owed this very unexpected visit.

"You wanted to speak to us about the Arnell case, Mr. Moss?" he asked, managing by a great effort of will to keep his voice level.

"Yes," answered Moss, a quiet smile spreading over his somewhat sombre face. "I thought that it was time I gave you the 'low-down' on what has been happening—as far as I can, that is."

Shelley was puzzled, and looked it. "Why did you decide to do this now, Mr. Moss?" he asked.

Again Moss smiled his almost inscrutable smile.

"Well," he said. "I reckon you'll think me about the biggest fool in Christendom when I tell you the silly joke

I fell for this afternoon. But the fact of the matter is that I'm very hard up, and I can't afford to throw away a chance of a possible piece of commission." He paused, and Shelley quickly interjected a question before the other could resume his rambling statement.

"I'm sorry, Mr. Moss," he said; "but I'm afraid I don't understand. You must begin at the beginning, and go straight through. That's the only way that we can get this business in order."

"Okay," said Moss. "I suppose I was telling the tale in a funny way. Little weakness of mine that I can't tell a tale straight through in a sensible way."

"Do your best," Shelley advised him; and he smiled.

"Well," he began, "I suppose the fact that I'm hard up, and in the hands of that old skinflint Victor Isaacs, really has nothing to do with the case."

"I wouldn't exactly say that, Mr. Moss," Shelley remarked dryly; "but, as a matter of fact, we know all about your financial position already."

"Do you, by Jove?" A rueful smile spread over the countenance of the young Jew. "What I was really saying all that for, though, was to explain that I am eager to get hold of any sort of job that will bring in a few quid—old Isaacs wants a bit of staving off; but I think if I could let him have fifty within the next few days he would wait a little longer."

"And then...?" Shelley was quietly insistent.

"Oh, I don't know." Moss shrugged his shoulders. "No doubt something or other would turn up, sooner or later," he said.

"Well, Mr. Micawber," smiled Shelley, "what precisely does all this lead up to?"

"This," said Moss. "I had a note this afternoon; and a pretty little wild-goose chase it's led me, too."

"A note?"

"Yes."

"What sort of note?"

"Well, this is it," said Moss, producing a letter from his pocket, and handing it over.

Shelley took it, handling it very gingerly, and removed it carefully from its envelope. Then he read it aloud, for the benefit of Cunningham, who had sat by almost open-mouthed at the preliminary conversation.

> "15, Berlin Square South, N.W.21" [he began]. "Dear Mr. Moss, Your name has been given me by a mutual friend, as one who can be relied on as a dealer in second-hand cars. I am told that you can usually get hold of something to suit anyone's requirements. Well, what I want is an Austin or Morris, about twelve horse-power, not older than 1934, price not above £75. Do you think that you can get hold of something for me? If you can, drive it around here this afternoon, as I am in rather a hurry to get fixed up, as I have to go on an important journey very shortly. If you cannot lay your hands on either of these, please bring along anything that you have anywhere near it, as it is very urgent that I should get fixed up soon. Please come this afternoon, as it is not sure at what times I shall be in for the rest of the week. Yours sincerely, Michael Baron."

"Well, what do you make of that, Inspector?" asked Moss.

"First of all," was Shelley's comment, "that Mr. Michael Baron was very anxious to get you out to—would it be Cricklewood?—this afternoon."

"Yes, damn him!" returned Moss. "And his blasted address doesn't exist."

"Doesn't it, now?" Shelley positively beamed at him. "That is indeed very gratifying."

"Gratifying, do you call it?" Moss objected. "I call it damned annoying. I went out there this afternoon, and spent hours looking for the blasted place. There's a Berlin Square right enough. As a matter of fact I knew it, and had been there before. But it's a square with only three sides, if you follow me. There's a Berlin Square North, East, and West, but no South."

Shelley positively purred. "Oh, very clever, very clever indeed," he murmured. "Just near enough to a real address to keep you puzzled, you see, Mr. Moss. The whole affair carefully thought out."

"Yes, but why?" asked Moss.

"Oh, that we shall find out in due course," said Shelley calmly.

"You think so?"

"I'm sure of it."

"Well, I'm glad of that, at any rate."

"In the meantime, Mr. Moss, I'd like to perform a little experiment," announced Shelley.

Moss looked alarmed. "Experiment?" he asked.

"Yes. I'd like to examine this letter for finger-prints. It's postmarked 'N.W.21,' I see, so the man took the trouble to go out there to post it." Shelley scribbled a note on a piece of paper, and then handed it to Cunningham, together with the letter.

"Take this to the finger-print department, Sergeant," he said, "and ask them if they can identify any of the prints on it with anyone in our records. This isn't a novice, and may well be due to an old hand at the game. I don't suppose he's left any prints, but the best people go astray at times."

"H'm." Moss did not look at all impressed at this suggestion, but Shelley quickly rounded on him.

"I shall require your finger-prints, of course, Mr. Moss," he said, "so that the finger-print department can eliminate them from the large number that will doubtless be on the envelope."

"Certainly," said Moss. "There will be no difficulty about that. Naturally, I don't raise any objection at this stage."

So he went through all the paraphernalia of inking fingers, one by one, and pressing them on the correct spaces on a marked and numbered card. One or two were slightly smudged, and had to be repeated, but at last Shelley announced himself satisfied with the results that they had attained. He rang a bell, and handed the card to a constable who had entered, telling him to take it down to the finger-print department for purposes of elimination in the specimen that he had just sent down.

"Tell them that these are the prints of Mr. Moss, the gentleman to whom the letter was addressed," he said. "And ask them to send up the result by Sergeant Cunningham as soon as available. I hope they hurry up, too. We have to go to the north of England tonight."

"North of England?" There was a question implicit in the tones of Moss's voice.

"Yes," said Shelley. "The gentleman who sent you that note—at any rate, I think he is responsible—kidnapped Miss Violet Arnell this afternoon. They are somewhere near Sheffield."

"Ah!" Moss was suddenly eager, his whole face expressing surprised comprehension of something that had hitherto been puzzling him. "So that explains the reason for the note."

"How?" Shelley could be laconic enough when his interest was aroused.

"I was to see Miss Arnell this afternoon or early evening—at least, that was the last arrangement that I had with her, I remember," Moss announced.

"Why?"

"Well," Moss hesitated. "We were sort of joint legatees of the old man," he explained. "And I was in a way suggesting to her...suggesting to her...that she might care to...care to..." His halting speech petered away into silence. Shelley smiled.

"You were suggesting to her that she should advance you a little of the money that was to be yours in any case eventually," he said.

"That's it," said Moss. "You see, I was in such a tight corner that I didn't know where to turn; and I thought that she might possibly see her way clear to do something about it."

"I follow," said Shelley. "Of course, Mr. Moss, I suppose it never occurred to you that your motives might be misconstrued?"

"What on earth do you mean?"

"I should have thought that my meaning was clear enough."

"Well, it isn't; so I wish you'd explain yourself, and not go talking in riddles," Moss objected.

"Well," said Shelley, and paused. It was now his turn to find things rather difficult to say.

"Carry on," said Moss with savage glee, experiencing considerable pleasure in being thus able to turn the tables on the famous detective.

"Miss Arnell is a very beautiful young lady, and an heiress to boot," snapped Shelley taking this conversational hurdle in his stride! "Also her fiancé is in prison—or was, until he was released early this evening."

"Are you suggesting that I was making up to Miss Arnell with the idea of marrying her?" shouted Moss.

"I was suggesting nothing," said Shelley, whose little experiment had succeeded. Moss was crimson with rage at the mere suggestion. This was no assumed temper; and

Shelley felt now fairly confident that the young Jew was completely innocent of criminal intent. The detective had put this offensive suggestion with the idea of seeing the reaction of his companion, for he felt sure that a guilty man would either have treated the idea as something merely to be smiled or sniggered at, or else as a serious idea which could be amicably discussed. A completely innocent man would be almost certain to react as Moss had done.

"Well," Moss stormed at him, "if you didn't suggest that, what the hell were you getting at, anyway? I tell you, you fellows think that you can get away with anything when you get people in here. Well, you can't as far as I'm concerned; and the sooner you get to know that the better it will be for you, and for all concerned."

"Now, that's all right, Mr. Moss," Shelley murmured, smoothing him down as best he could. "Please forget that anything of the sort was ever said. I quite see that it was impossible that you could have done, to have contemplated doing, anything of the sort."

"That's all right then," murmured Moss in slightly mollified tones.

"Good," remarked Shelley. "But what I want to know, Mr. Moss, is this: who could have done it? After all, even though he is a criminal, who has, for some unknown reason, kidnapped Miss Arnell, he must be known to you personally in some way."

"Why do you think that?"

"That letter," Shelley pointed out. "It shows a pretty considerable knowledge of your habits, of your job, and of what you do. After all, one must know you fairly well to be aware that you can fish up a second-hand car of a particular make, year, and price. Or don't you think so?"

Moss considered this for a few moments. "I don't know," he said at length. "After all, I am pretty well known in the world of second-hand cars, you know. I must have deal-ings with a score of people a month—or more, even. Some months I might have dealings with as many as fifty people, and each of those fifty would have some friends to whom they'd mention my name. You know—'Got a decent second-hand car from a chap called Moss'—that sort of thing."

"But that's different from knowing your private address and so on," Shelley objected. "After all, the letter was addressed to you personally at your home address. Don't forget that."

"I'm in the 'phone book," Moss reminded him.

"Yes, that's so," said Shelley. He felt almost "stumped." The thing did, on reflection, seem almost inexplicable, unless the man was someone who knew Moss well, he thought; and yet each of the little points, which in sum seemed to mean so much, had a perfectly natural explanation. But to the trained mind of the detective the explanations some-how did not quite ring true. There seemed to be something forced, something vaguely unnatural about them. He could not manage to lay his finger on any particular spot in the explanation which was wrong; and yet, taken as a whole it was all wrong. The detective of wide experience gets these occasional "hunches," and it was one of Shelley's deepest feelings that they rarely proved wrong. He felt perfectly sure that in this instance he was correct; and that the crimi-nal, whoever he might eventually turn out to be, would be someone well known to Moss.

Before he had time to put this matter before Moss, however, Cunningham returned, his face one broad beam-ing smile.

"Hullo, Cunningham," he said with a smile which answered that on Cunningham's countenance. "You look as if you'd picked up a five-pound note. That must mean that you have some good news for us."

"Indeed, it does, sir."

"Well, don't waste time, man. Tell us all about it. Fire ahead."

"The finger-prints on the envelope were entirely Mr. Moss's, and someone's who we couldn't identify," said Cunningham.

"Right. I understand your meaning, even if your grammar isn't all it might be," smiled Shelley. "Probably the postman is the gentleman whom you couldn't identify."

"Yes, sir. That's what we thought."

"And the letter, man. Don't keep us waiting." Shelley was clearly on tenterhooks.

"The letter had a distinct thumb-print on the back," said Cunningham with a smile, "which was identified in the department."

"Who was it?"

"Wallace. J. K. Wallace," returned Cunningham.

Shelley looked puzzled for a moment, and then his memory became its usual efficient self. "J. K. Wallace," he said reflectively. "That was the man who did ten years for a cheque-book fraud, isn't it?"

"Yes, sir," said Cunningham. "That was before my time at the Yard, though."

"He came out about ten years ago," said Shelley.

"How old would he be?" asked Cunningham.

Again Shelley reflected for a moment, and then: "Oh, not much over forty," he said. "He was a very young fellow, not much over twenty when he was convicted. Ten years in prison, ten years out. Yes, that would make him fortyish now."

Then he turned to Moses Moss. "Did you ever come across a man called Wallace?" he asked. "Moderate height, clean-shaven with a blue chin. Thick black hair, close-cropped?"

Now came perhaps the greatest shock which Shelley had hitherto sustained in this case. Blankly, his face showing total ignorance, Moss shook his head. "No. Never met him in my life," he said.

"And what do we do now?" asked Shelley.

Nobody enlightened him.

Chapter XVII

An Astounding Offer

Violet was terrified, but she was firmly determined not to show it. Whatever might be the remarkable offer which this strange man was going to make, she steeled herself to meet it with real stoicism. She had nearly reached the end of her tether, and her nerves were ragged and on edge; but she kept a firm grip on herself, being resolved not to show the man the terror that had laid hold upon her.

He smiled an oily smile, and settled himself on the edge of the bed. She was standing in the middle of the room.

"Won't you take a seat, my dear young lady?" he said, leering at her unpleasantly.

"Thank you," she replied in the stiffest, most formal tones she could command, "but I think that I prefer to stand."

"As you like," he murmured with a shrug of his shoulders; "but what I have to say to you may well take some considerable time, and I feel sure that you will be tired with standing all that time. Are you certain that you will not sit down? Honestly, it is entirely for your own good that I suggest it. There is no ulterior motive in the suggestion. I can assure you of that."

There was still a queer little trace of foreign accent in his speech, and Violet kept asking herself what was his nationality. She could not, however, make up her mind about the matter—and in any case, she told herself, what on earth did that matter?

"If you insist," she said, "I will sit down. But I ask you, please, to be as quick as you can. I have no desire to have a long interview."

She found herself unconsciously slipping into the stiff, formal phraseology, as if she felt that by thus keeping him conversationally at a distance, she would be able to ward off whatever danger might be threatening her.

"Well, neither have I," he admitted. "I say that quite frankly. But I fear that what I have to say—the proposition I am going to put before you—requires a certain amount of explanation, and cannot be disposed of in two or three minutes, as it would seem you wish."

"Tell me what you want, and then go," said Violet imperiously, and he grinned. There was a little more humour in his grin now. It was not, she fancied, quite as grim and menacing as had been the smiles that he had showered on her so plenteously earlier in the interview.

"As you like," he said, spreading his hands in quite a French fashion; and then, without more ado, he began to say what he wanted to tell her.

"You are, I understand," he began, "engaged to be married to Mr. Harry Baker."

"Yes."

"Are you—what they would say, very much in love with that young gentleman?"

"Yes."

"You still think that he will be set free by the so foolish police, eh?"

"Yes."

"And you still think that when he is thus set free you will marry him, eh?"

"Yes."

"You are not in a very chatty mood, are you?" he asked, leaning towards her and grinning up into her face.

"I am not," returned Violet. "And I would remind you, sir, that this interview is not of my seeking. I understood that you wished to put some sort of proposition before me. I did not know that you were intending to cross-examine me as to certain private matters which are, after all, entirely my own affair."

"Haughty!" he exclaimed, and chuckled loudly.

"It was necessary," he went on, "that I should know certain things about your private life, my dear Miss Arnell, before I went on to put this proposition before you. I hope that you understand what I mean; and that you do not think that all those questions were just pieces of studied insolence on my part."

"I'm afraid I don't understand in the least," said Violet hotly. "I haven't any idea what you are driving at; and, if you don't soon explain what you want me to do, I shall begin to think that you are merely trying to waste my time—though to what end, I simply can't imagine at all."

Again he chuckled. "I do not waste your time, my dear young lady," he said. "Nor, for that matter, do I waste my own, which I would guess is probably a good deal more valuable than yours."

"Explain yourself, then, and don't beat about the bush in this way," said Violet.

"I will," said he, and paused. He seemed to find his mysterious proposition, whatever it might be, exceedingly difficult to put into words, and Violet found herself gazing out of the window, admiring the lovely shades of brown and gold which were there. Again she found herself wondering precisely where she was; and she put her thought, almost unwittingly, into words.

"I wonder," she asked, "if you would mind telling me precisely where I am?"

"Certainly, I will tell you where you are," he replied, somewhat surprisingly. "You are in the spare bedroom of a little cottage that I keep up here for my own use in moments of emergency."

"But where is 'up here'?" Violet persisted, stubbornly intent, now that she had managed to get him to talk on this subject, on gaining her point.

"I see no harm," he said quietly, "why you should not know. You are on the Yorkshire moors, not very far from Sheffield."

"But this is lovely countryside," she objected, and he smiled.

"You have the usual south-country idea that Yorkshire is one big, smoky, dirty city," he said. "Sheffield is less than fifteen miles away. You seem to find that difficult to believe, do you not?"

She nodded.

"Well," he said, "if and when you get free, you just look on a map of England in an atlas, and find a little town called Penistone. You are about a mile or two away from there at this moment."

"Penistone?" Violet thought deeply for a moment or two. "I've never heard of it before," she added.

"I do not suppose for one moment that you have," he agreed. "Possibly it has not heard of you." And he chuckled again at his footling little joke.

"But," said Violet, "will you please get on with your explanation of this mysterious proposition which you were so anxious to put before me not so very long ago?"

"Ah! I had almost forgotten, in the excitement of our little geographical discussion," he said. "But do not forget, my dear Miss Arnell, that it was you who led us off that pleasant little bypath of conversation."

"Please," said Violet. "I am tired of this. Tell me what it is that you wish me to do."

"One or two more questions, if you do not mind," he added, and then, before she had time to raise any objections, he went on hurriedly: "You have said that you are very much in love with Mr. Harry Baker. But what if he were found guilty of murder—as he almost certainly will be? What if he is hanged? What will be your feelings about marriage then, my dear young lady?"

Violet shuddered. She had to admit to herself that it seemed only too likely that Harry would be hanged. In spite of the discoveries which Mr. Fairhurst had made at her instigation, there was, she knew, still a very strong case against Harry; and it might well be that, even with the assistance of the best counsel who could be obtained, he would be unable to prove his innocence.

"I don't think that it is in the least likely that he will be found guilty," she announced bravely.

"We shall see about that, Miss Arnell," returned her captor. "I think it only too likely that he will. There is an exceedingly strong case against him; he has acted most suspiciously, and, when once the police lay their hands on a man, they are not very ready to let him go."

"But in any case, I do not see what on earth is the use of all this discussion of something that will in all probability never happen," Violet objected.

"Take it as something purely hypothetical, Miss Arnell," urged the man. "I assure you that your attitude on this matter is highly important."

Violet suppressed an inclination to giggle. In spite of the terrible seriousness of her position, the thought of discussing the love-affair which had given her such joy—and above all, of discussing it with a man she scarcely knew; whose very name, even, she had never heard—seemed crazily absurd.

"What do you want to know?" she asked.

"Merely what would be your view of marriage if Mr. Baker did not exist," he explained.

"If Harry died, I should have no desire to marry," she said with quiet dignity. "He is the only man I have ever cared for at all deeply; and I do not suppose that I shall ever again love anyone as I love him."

"So? That is rather a pity," he commented.

"Why a pity?" asked Violet. "After all, as I said just now, it is in the last degree unlikely that he should be found guilty; so really the question of what I should want to do in the event of his death does not arise."

"But," he said quietly, "you have to put Mr. Harry Baker right out of your life."

"Put him out of my life?" Violet laughed aloud. "My dear sir, you don't know what you are talking about. Harry and I will be married within a few months—as soon as we decently can, without showing any sort of disrespect to my father's memory."

"Alive or dead," he persisted, "you will not marry Harry Baker."

"And who am I to marry, pray?" she asked, with some hauteur, the question being rather a rhetorical one than one where an answer was either required or expected.

"Mr. Moses Moss," answered the other, and again she laughed aloud.

"If Mr. Moss were the only man on earth, I should go to my grave an old maid," she said. "Besides, why should Mr. Moss want to marry me?"

"I do not know," said her captor, "that Mr. Moss has even considered marrying you. But I do know that he will do so when I order him to."

"When you order him to?"

"Precisely."

"But what power have you that you can order other people's lives?" she asked, and she saw the dangerous glitter of madness come into his eyes.

"I have the greatest power on earth, my dear Miss Arnell," he said. "The power that no man or woman dare defy or neglect."

"And that is?"

"That is the power of money."

Violet was now between tears and laughter; but she still felt that she must argue with this man, lunatic though she was now sure that he was.

"I fear that you have not enough money to make me marry Mr. Moss," she objected. "I would not marry him for all the money in the world. I have told you that I am very deeply in love with Harry Baker, and if I cannot marry him I shall never marry at all."

"That is as it may be," he said. "You now have great strength of will—or so you think. We will see what a little solitary confinement will do."

"Am I to be kept prisoner here indefinitely?" she asked indignantly.

"No," he replied with a smile. "You will not be kept here indefinitely, my dear Miss Arnell. I could afford to spare neither the time nor the money that would be necessary for such a course of action."

"Then what is to happen when you realise that I am not going to give in to your outrageous demands?" asked Violet. "And you know you will be compelled to realise that sooner or later."

"If you prove so obstinate that there is obviously no moving you, my dear young lady," he said in tones as sweet as his words were harsh, "then you will have to be otherwise disposed of."

"What do you mean?"

"Need I be more explicit?"

"I certainly think you do. I haven't the foggiest notion of what you are getting at."

"Just think it over, Miss Arnell. I think that if you get that obstinate little brain of yours to work you will soon see the answer to the problem."

With that he was gone. He whisked himself quickly through the door, and shut it behind him. Violet heard the key turning in the lock.

She sat perfectly still for some minutes, going over and over in her mind the interview which had passed. Of course, she told herself, it was obvious enough what they were after—her money! And Moses Moss, in spite of what the man had said, was clearly in on the whole affair. Clearly he had forged her father's will; and had made it apparently benefit her, with the idea that he should marry her, and so get hold of her father's great fortune. And worse still to think of—Moses Moss and this nameless horror of a gaoler had murdered her father and the poor, unfortunate Dr. Crocker as well. And they had planned the whole affair so that she should be made free of Harry; "framing-up" the case so that Harry should be found guilty.

It was all perfectly plain. And if she did not fall in with their plans she too would be murdered in her turn. The situation seemed perfectly hopeless, and she almost gave way to her grief. Here she was, up in Yorkshire that is, if the information which the man had given her was correct; and there seemed no reason why it should not be—and there was absolutely nothing to point the way of the detectives towards here, even if they as much as suspected that she had been kidnapped.

Then she had a pleasant thought. After all, Henry Fairhurst was on her side. He was not such a fool as he looked; and he had promised to telephone the news to her when he had talked over the matter of the forged will with Shelley.

Would he think that there was something wrong when he found that she was not in? Would he have the sense to go back at once to the Yard and tell them that she had mysteriously disappeared? And would the detectives have enough skill to trace her?

These questions, of course, were quite unanswerable; and yet she found her mind going over them again and again.

She felt tired. The long interview with her captor had been more exhausting than she had realised at the time. She would lie down on the bed for a few minutes, she thought. She would not go to sleep, of course. It would be perfectly ridiculous to go to sleep in broad daylight like this. But it was so pleasantly restful just to close her eyes for a minute and to relax…In a minute she was asleep.

Chapter XVIII

Northward Ho!

"This is all very mysterious, Mr. Moss," said Shelley, slowly recovering from his astonishment that the young Jew did not even know the man who had presumably sent him the note.

"I'll say it is," Moss agreed.

"I'd give a lot, Mr. Moss," added Shelley, "to know precisely who it is that is holding Miss Arnell prisoner—or who has, at any rate, kidnapped her and taken her off to the north of England in this cavalier fashion. It would be interesting to know who he is."

"Sorry I can't help you there, sir," said Moss. "But it looks as if catching that man is your pigeon. Don't think I can be much use to you, really. Guess I'll get home to bed—that is, if you don't want me to stay here. I presume I'm not under suspicion; or under arrest; or anything like that." And he laughed, though the laugh was not a particularly impressive effort; it spoke bewilderment, fear, and—so Shelley thought—hostility.

"No, I don't think we want you to stay in attendance any longer, Mr. Moss," said Shelley. "You've been perfectly frank with us, as far as we know; and I see no reason why you should not go home to your bed. Only don't leave London without letting us know."

"Thank you, sir," replied Moss with every indication of profound gratitude.

"That's all right. Don't thank me. Thank the lucky stars that made you keep that letter and its envelope. If it hadn't been for that we might well have suspected you," Shelley told him and then, holding out his hand in a friendly manner, wished him good night.

As soon as the young man was gone, however, his manner changed instantly. From the quiet, almost languid friend, Shelley became the detective on duty, alert, active, and without scruple when pursuing his quarry. He picked up a telephone from his desk, and spoke a few incisive words into its receiver.

"Jim?" he asked. "Good. A young man has just left my office—handsome young Jew—and I want him shadowed night and day. Two best men you have, put on his track. Don't let him budge an inch without a shadow."

A question came from the other end of the wire—a question Shelley had expected—and he answered. "Dangerous? No; I shouldn't really think so; but you never know. And there's just an outside chance that he may be a murderer. See? So put the best men you have on his trail; and tell them to report back immediately if he attempts to leave London; and to arrest him on suspicion if it looks like flight, and they haven't time to get through to headquarters. Got that? Good." And he slammed the receiver down, and wheeled round in his chair to face a thoughtful-looking Cunningham.

"Well, Cunningham? What do you think of our Mr. Moss?"

Cunningham shrugged his shoulders non-committally.

"Very difficult to say, sir," he replied.

"I agree. That's why I'm taking no chances. I don't know the identity of the lunatic whom we're shortly going to chase in the north of England," added Shelley, "but, as there is at any rate a possibility that he's an accomplice of Moses Moss, I'm taking no chances with that gentleman. I don't want him—if he is in on this—to slip through our fingers while we're chasing the other fellow. See?"

Cunningham saw.

"Now," added Shelley briskly. "Sheffield. I fear that Mr. Moss has taken up rather more time than I intended. So we shall have to find other trains. What ones are there?"

Again Cunningham scanned the time-table. "There's one at twelve-fifteen, sir," he announced at length. "Reaches Sheffield at four-thirty a.m. How will that do?"

"Have to do, I suppose," Shelley grumbled. "One of these days, Cunningham, I am going to get a decent job, where I don't have to miss sleep. Thank Heaven I'm not married, anyway. What does your wife think of your spending so much time away from home?" Then, without waiting for a reply to this purely rhetorical question, he swept on: "Anyhow, we must try to get a spot of sleep in the train if we can. I guess we shan't get much tomorrow."

Cunningham made for the door and hurried out, preparing to get the car which he knew would be demanded to get them to St. Pancras.

Shelley followed in more leisurely fashion, stopping at the finger-print department to get a photograph, now developed, fixed, and dried, of the prints of J. K. Wallace, the ex-criminal who had so mysteriously appeared in this case at such a late stage, and whom, even yet, they were totally unable to identify.

At the door of the car he was stopped by an excited figure, bowler hat all awry, pince-nez absurdly on the tip of his nose.

"Hullo, Mr. Fairhurst," he said. "Sorry I can't stop now. In a hurry. We're on the track of Miss Arnell, and we have to catch a train."

"But, Mr. Shelley," panted the little man, who had obviously been hurrying, "I want to talk to you about this case."

"Sorry, Mr. Fairhurst," snapped Shelley. "Any other time. At the moment I'm busy."

"It is important!"

"Sure?"

"Yes, Mr. Shelley."

Shelley paused for a moment, thinking of some way out of this difficulty. True, Fairhurst had brought them information of some importance previously, and it was possible that he had some sort of material clue which he was now trying to put before them. Then he saw the solution.

"If you think this information is vital, Mr. Fairhurst," he said, "jump in." He indicated the waiting car, at the wheel of which a policeman sat impassively.

"Come with you?" Mr. Fairhurst was very excited at the prospect.

"If you think you can be any help to us in this case." Shelley was carefully non-committal.

"Yes!" Mr. Fairhurst's eyes shone, his pince-nez slipped a degree nearer the tip of his nose, and the tilt of his hat became more unconsciously rakish than ever. "Yes!" he repeated. "I will come with you to wherever you are going, Mr. Shelley; and I hope that I may be of some assistance in bringing this rascal to heel."

Speedily, silently, and efficiently the police car sped along the Strand, up deserted Kingsway, and so to St. Pancras. Soon they were comfortably tucked away in the seclusion of a first-class compartment; speeding through the sleeping suburbs towards the north.

Shelley produced his old briar pipe, filled it with rank tobacco, and lit up. Then he turned to the little man who had thus unexpectedly joined their party, and asked him what was the important information which he had to give them.

"Moses Moss," announced Mr. Fairhurst in dramatic tones, "is in London!"

Cunningham emitted a disgusted grunt. "Is that all you have to tell us, Mr. Fairhurst?" he asked in tones of bitter contempt.

"Isn't that enough?" asked Henry. "I was walking along the Strand when I saw him. You could have knocked me down with a feather. There he was, as bold as brass, just marching along the Strand as if he owned the place."

"I suppose," remarked Shelley, "that you didn't see a shortish, middle-aged man with a tweed coat and a black Homburg hat, a few yards behind him?"

"No," said Mr. Fairhurst. "Who was he?"

"Detective-Sergeant Pinto, of the Criminal Investigation Department, New Scotland Yard," answered Shelley with a superior smile.

"One of your men?" Henry Fairhurst looked completely bewildered.

"One of our men."

"Then you knew all about it?"

"We knew all about it."

"But why am I coming to Sheffield with you?"

"Why, indeed?"

Henry was worried at the thought that he had mulcted the tax-payers of Great Britain of the price of one first-class return ticket from St. Pancras to Sheffield; and Shelley was vaguely annoyed that he had somehow managed to burden himself with an outsider at this vital stage of his investigation. Still, it couldn't be helped; and he would have to send him back to London at the first opportunity, on the first available train.

"I suppose," he asked, thinking that he could, after all, be sensible, and try if Henry had any information on the subject which was uppermost in his mind, "that you never chanced to come across a man called J. K. Wallace?"

"Why," was the surprising answer, "what has old J. K. been doing now?"

"Mr. Fairhurst," Shelley burst out, "you are a gift from the gods. Again and again you have brought me some information, and this time you have the best of the lot. You actually *knew* Mr. J. K. Wallace?"

"Of course I did. It was many years ago. He was..." Henry hesitated, as if in some embarrassment; and then went on bravely, taking his courage firmly in both hands: "He was at one time one of my best friends; but I disapproved of his way of life and we quarrelled, so that in recent years I have not met him."

Shelley and Cunningham exchanged significant glances. This, they told each other, was the greatest stroke of luck that they had managed to secure.

"Tell me," said Mr. Shelley, "how did you meet the man in the first instance?"

"It was," answered Henry, "in the Reading Room of the British Museum, some eight or nine years ago."

"H'm," commented Shelley. "Not long after he was released from Dartmoor."

"Yes. He told me all about that," said Henry; and Shelley laughed.

"I doubt if he told you all," the detective remarked. "Did he tell you, for instance, that he was sent to prison for complicity in a most ingenious fraud, perpetrated jointly on a bank and an insurance company?"

"I must say," Henry admitted, "that when I found out a little about his way of life I began to wonder if there might be something of that sort. He swore that he was innocent, of course. He said that he was 'framed-up'—at least, I think that was the phrase—by a gang who wanted to get rid of him. I suppose it was a complete untruth; was it not?"

Shelley inclined his head gravely. "I'm afraid he seriously deceived you, Mr. Fairhurst," he admitted.

"I suppose it was my own fault for succumbing so easily to the blandishments of a stranger in the British Museum Library that day," Henry said. "But you see so many interesting people meet there that one somehow feels there is a sort of freemasonry of learning there."

Shelley looked thoughtful. "Yes; I suppose there is something of that kind of feeling," he said. "Just the same way as I feel a fellow-feeling for a policeman anywhere. Yes; I see that."

"But it was not so, Mr. Shelley," complained Henry. "You see, to begin with we used to have occasional meals together; and he used to tell me all about the dreadful times he had at Dartmoor; and what wicked men there were there; and all that sort of thing."

Shelley nodded. "I understand," he said.

"Well," Henry continued. "That was how it began; but after it had been going on for a month or two I realised that I always paid for those meals. And, if I happened to suggest a drink, it always happened, after I had paid for one, that he had some highly important business elsewhere, and so was not able to stay to pay for his. All little things, but they began to get on my nerves."

Shelley again nodded sympathetically.

"And then," Henry went on, conscious of an attentive audience, "he began to borrow money from me. Only small sums, you understand. A shilling now, and half a crown next week."

The train roared on through the night; and Henry paused as it passed into a tunnel, the reverberations being too loud to allow easy conversation. Shelley seized the opportunity to refill his pipe, and to get it going again, disregarding the coughs of Henry Fairhurst as the rank smoke puffed out into the compartment.

"This borrowing business," Henry resumed as soon as the tunnel was past, "continued for a long time. At first he paid the money back regularly, then there were occasions when I had to remind him that he had not paid me back. It was a most disagreeable affair, I can assure you, Mr. Shelley."

Shelley made sympathetic noises once more, and said: "Go on, Mr. Fairhurst. All this is most interesting; and you will understand its value in the present case when I tell you something later on. For the moment I want all the information about Mr. Wallace that I can conveniently lay my hands on."

Henry almost purred with pleasure. "The present case, did I understand you to say, Mr. Shelley?" he asked. "Well, all this is very gratifying; very gratifying indeed. I hope that I shall be able to tell you something which will be of real assistance in this case."

"I am sure you will, sir," answered Shelley gravely. "Do go on with your story. I am sure that Cunningham is just as eager as I am to hear the rest of it; and how the unfortunate affair ended."

"Well," said Henry and paused irresolutely for a moment. "He went on borrowing more and more money from me, still paying it back with—shall I say a little pressure from time to time? I didn't like to refuse the poor chap. He always had such a good excuse for wanting a little cash, just to tide him over a difficult time."

"He would," said Shelley grimly.

"This went on, as I said," continued Henry, "for some months. One week he would pay me back half a crown and borrow five shillings. The next week he would borrow another five shillings; and, after asking him several times, I should recover the ten shillings a month later. I trust that I make myself perfectly clear, Inspector?"

"Perfectly clear, Mr. Fairhurst," returned Shelley. "I only wish that all the witnesses we had to deal with could express themselves half as clearly."

Again Henry preened himself with satisfaction. Such praise from the great men of Scotland Yard, he told himself, did not come everyone's way.

"Once, however, he borrowed five pounds from me. He was, he informed me, on the point of being thrown out of his lodgings, as he owed several weeks' rent." Henry paused, and looked at his listeners to see if they had any remarks to make with regard to this somewhat surprising proceeding on the part of Mr. Wallace.

As no comment was forthcoming, however, he went on: "I asked him countless times to return this five pounds, as, though I am by no means a poor man, Inspector, five pounds is more money than I care to throw down a drain, so to speak."

"I quite understand," said Shelley.

"But," went on Henry, "he showed no desire whatever to pay this perfectly just debt. Every time I asked him for the money, he had some excuse to make. He would have some other debt which was more urgent, as his creditor had threatened to issue a summons if the cash wasn't paid by a certain date. Or there would be some books which he had to buy for the literary research he was engaged upon—"

"Literary research work?" Shelley swiftly interrupted. "I never heard that Mr. Wallace was interested in any sort of literature."

"Oh, he was exceedingly well read. He knew, especially, all about the lesser Elizabethan dramatists…" Henry's voice slowly died away. A look of sudden comprehension came over his face. "Is that the connection with the death of Professor Arnell?" he asked in excited tones.

"It may be one connection," Shelley admitted. "But a more or less accidental one, I imagine. Probably it was some such item of knowledge which suggested the way in which the murder was carried out."

"Then he is the murderer?" Henry was really excited now. "Yes."

"But…but…I don't see what he has to do with Professor Arnell," complained Henry.

"Neither do I," said Shelley. "I know how it was done. He probably knew Professor Arnell as a fellow-worker in the British Museum Library. He inserted the poisoned sweet in the packet which the Professor used to leave on his table in the library as he went to the central desk to hand in his tickets requesting books."

"And Dr. Crocker?"

"He was enticed up from Oxford on a pledge of secrecy; probably by a forged note asking him to come to meet Professor Arnell, or, more likely, someone who could assist him to show up Professor Arnell as a fraud."

"That's possible. But what about Harry Baker?"

"Another decoy letter. Harry said that a letter had brought him there. You see, the decoy letter seems to be a favourite system of his. He used one—if what Moses Moss says is true—to get Moss away from Miss Arnell last evening so that he could bring off his little kidnapping trick."

"But what on earth is the reason for all this?" asked Henry in astonishment.

"That's what puzzles me, too," Shelley admitted. "I can't make up my mind what is the explanation. My feeling is that Mr. Wallace has disguised himself in some way, and has been leading, so to speak, a double life. We may already have come across him in some other capacity in this case, so that we should know, could we only 'spot' his present identity, what he was after. Until we can link up the two halves of Mr. Wallace, there is no chance of doing anything in the matter."

"Did you ever see him in the old days?" asked Henry.

"No. That's the trouble. If I did the case would probably be solved," answered Shelley. "But you did not finish your story. What happened finally in your little business dealings with the gentleman?"

"Oh, when I couldn't recover my five pounds, I wrote to him and told him that I wanted nothing more to do with him."

"Wisest thing to do," was Shelley's comment on this.

"I also said that I was compelled to refuse his invitation to spend a week-end with him at his cottage in Penistone, and—"

"What?" Shelley almost jumped out of his seat as he yelled the question. "Did you say his cottage at *Penistone?*"

Henry looked puzzled. "Yes; what of it?" he asked.

"Have you any idea where Penistone is?" the detective asked.

Henry shook his head.

"Somewhere in the West Riding," he said. "That's all I knew."

"Less than twelve miles from Sheffield," said Shelley. "And it was in Sheffield that he was seen with Miss Arnell yesterday evening."

"Heavens!" Henry looked amazed. "Then…then…it is the last lap."

"The last lap," said Shelley with a grim smile.

The train roared on through the darkness. Sparks flew thickly from its chimney, and the other passengers, unconscious of the messenger of the law who was speeding in it towards the place where he was to meet a murderer, did their best to sleep.

Chapter XIX

The Chase Begins

Sheffield railway station is not an especially attractive place at any time. At four o'clock in the morning, with lights shining dimly through the gloom, Shelley thought that it looked the most dismal place on earth.

They were met by an excited police inspector, who began talking in quick, sharp sentences as soon as they had reached the car which was waiting outside the station.

"Don't know where they've gone yet," he said. "Seems they went out Barnsley way. Out over the moors, that is. We've got a crowd of men on the trail. News soon, I hope."

Shelley looked at him for a moment with a twinkling eye.

"Might they be going to a place called Penistone?" he asked.

The local man gazed at him in amazement. "How did you hear about that, now?" he asked. "For that's roughly the direction that they would be going. About twelve miles out. They'd be there long ago."

"That's cheerful hearing, anyway," answered Shelley, with quite a happy smile that belied the sarcastic tones of his voice. "The fact is that we have a gentleman with us"—he indicated Henry Fairhurst—"who knew the man in the past."

"Is that so, now?" The local man indicated the liveliest interest.

"Yes," returned Shelley. "And, what's more, he was once invited to spend a week-end with the rascal at Penistone."

"Eh, that's grand!"

"Looks as if we're pretty close on his trail, I think; don't you?" asked Shelley.

"Ay; it does that," responded the other heartily. His name, it seemed, was Bowes; and he had been in the Sheffield Constabulary for more years than he cared to reckon. At any rate, Shelley thought, he would prove a very useful ally; for he claimed to know the countryside like the back of his hand—a very useful asset in such a case as the present one, since it seemed probable that they would have to do a good deal of chasing and tracking over the hills.

"The only difficulty," Shelley explained, "is that Mr. Fairhurst was never given the address—or if he was he has completely forgotten it, since it was eight or nine years ago."

"Was it in Penistone itself, or somewhere outside the town?" asked Inspector Bowes, turning towards Henry and addressing him for the first time.

"That's the trouble," answered Henry, smiling. "I really can't remember anything about the house. You see, it wasn't as if I ever visited it. It was only that I was once invited there, and I never accepted the invitation. I've never been in Penistone, and I shouldn't recognise the house if I saw it. It's all," he concluded, "rather difficult, and I'm only sorry that I can't help more."

"So is Mr. Shelley, I'll be bound," said Inspector Bowes.

"Oh, I don't know," smiled Shelley. "After all, we've been very lucky to get hold of the information which Mr. Fairhurst has already given us, you know."

"Have you got any idea at all about this place?" asked Inspector Bowes, but then interrupted before Henry had time to reply. "Here we are at the station, Mr. Shelley. May as well make ourselves comfortable in front of a fire, as talk out here in the cold, you know."

"Agreed," said Shelley. So they left the car, walked over the cobbled pavement into a cosy little room with a roaring fire in the grate.

"Now, Mr. Fairhurst," said Inspector Bowes, when they had settled themselves down in this room, pipes well alight, and feet inside the fender. "I think you were just going to answer that question of mine about whether you had any idea at all about this place."

Henry smiled weakly. "But in a very disappointing way, I fear, Inspector," he said. "You see, I don't know anything at all about it."

Shelley quickly interposed: "But that really shouldn't matter much, you know. I imagine that youngish men with black beards aren't so common in Yorkshire as they are—say, in Chelsea."

"That's true," returned Bowes. "Still, I'd say it'll be a matter of some hours before we get anywhere at all. You know, our men, patrolling the moors here, are bound to be few and far between; so that it may be some time before any news comes through."

"What do you suggest we do?" asked Shelley.

"I should say a bit of sleep wouldn't do you any harm," replied the other.

"That's true," returned Shelley. "I must say that for my part I'm dog-tired after all this rushing about the country. What do you say, folks?"

Cunningham and Henry Fairhurst agreed.

"Sorry I can't offer you a bedroom," the local man went on; "but there are plenty of cushions about; and, with the chairs and the couch, you should be able to make yourselves comfortable for a few hours."

"Quite," said Shelley.

"I'll leave you, then."

"Yes. But let us know the moment any news comes through."

"Ay; I'll do that all right, never fear."

Bowes left them; and they settled down to try to get a few hours' badly needed sleep. In somewhat incongruous positions, Henry Fairhurst curled up like a small boy in a huge leather arm-chair, Cunningham with his feet stretched before the fire, his bulky body compressed within the confining arms of another chair, and Shelley on the couch, his feet hanging over the arm at one end and his head over the other. In spite of all these handicaps, however, they managed to get a little sleep, even though it was somewhat disturbed slumber.

Then Shelley woke suddenly, shaking himself with surprise and gazing around him with a puzzled frown. The effort of realising precisely where he was had, at first, been too much for him; but he soon came to his senses, and made up his mind what had happened. But what had wakened him? He looked up and saw Henry Fairhurst, the stubble of twenty-four hours' growth looking strangely out of place on his usually immaculate chin. Henry had gripped Shelley by the shoulder and was shaking him vigorously.

"What's the matter?" Shelley asked sleepily.

"Are you awake, Mr. Shelley?"

"Yes. What's the matter?"

"I've remembered something important."

"Important? What about?"

"About Wallace's house."

"Wallace's house? In Penistone?"

"Yes."

Shelley struggled into an upright position, rubbed his eyes with a gesture curiously reminiscent of a sleepy child, and looked Henry Fairhurst straight in the face. At last he was fully awake, and prepared to receive whatever this important information might be.

"What is it you've remembered?" he asked briskly. "Shoot!"

"I have been lying awake," answered Mr. Fairhurst, "and trying to recall the name of the house."

"So you did know the name of the house once?"

"Naturally. Wallace wrote to me from there when he asked me to come down for the week-end that time."

"Good. And could you remember it?" Shelley wished with all his heart that Henry would come to the point a little more quickly, and would not so "beat about the bush."

"I've only got the vaguest memory," answered Henry. "All that I can remember is that 'Black' came somewhere in it."

"Black?" Shelley was puzzled again.

"Yes. It may have been called Black House, or Black Manor, or even Black Farm."

Shelley looked thoughtful. "That all you can remember about it?" he asked.

Henry was very apologetic. "I'm afraid it is," he admitted.

"H'm. Might be helpful or might not," Shelley announced. "Still, there's only one way to be sure. We must ask Bowes if he knows of anywhere in or near Penistone that is called Black something."

"It might even be Black-something House," suggested Henry, not particularly helpfully. Shelley snorted.

But he went to the door, opened it, and looked around. It was now broad daylight, and in the outer room of the Sheffield Police Station there were several constables on duty.

"Inspector Bowes about?" Shelley asked the nearest one of these men.

"Ay! Do you want to see him?" asked the policeman.

"Right away."

"I'll get him." And get him the constable did, for in less than a minute Bowes was with them again.

Shelley explained: "Mr. Fairhurst's memory has played him a nasty trick."

"H'm." A non-committal grunt was Bowes's only contribution to the discussion at this stage. Typically Yorkshire phlegm characterised him, and he was resolute in showing no emotion, even when these crazy folk from London (as he thought of them) began to get excited and worked up with what they so fondly imagined was important information.

"Yes." Shelley saw that he would have to explain the whole affair before any information would be granted him. "He remembered that the house was called Black something. It may be Black Manor or anything. All that Mr. Fairhurst remembers is that the word 'Black' comes into the title somewhere. Now, do you know of anywhere in or near Penistone that has such a name?"

"Let me see, now." Inspector Bowes winkled up his ruddy brow in the effort at thought. He scratched his head and muttered to himself, his face growing more and more blank as the moments passed. Then he turned to them again.

"Can't say I remember any house or farm of the name," he said. "But then you must recall that I'm a Sheffield lad, born and bred. Maybe somebody from Penistone would be able to tell more than I can about the places there. It may be some sort of place of the name there—but it might happen that I had never heard of it, you see."

"Have you any Penistone men here?" asked Shelley. "It would save time; we shouldn't have to hunt around Penistone when we got there."

"That's true," admitted Bowes, and thought once more. This time, however, his brow quickly cleared, and he smiled cheerily. "As it happens, we have," he said. "There's a Constable Cartwright. He's only just joined the force, as it happens, and his home is in Penistone, so that he'll be able to tell us where the place is, if anybody could."

"Is he on duty at the moment?" asked Shelley eagerly.

"Ay," answered the other, without a trace of excitement. "I'll just call him in, and you can question him if you want to."

Cartwright, on being called in, turned out to be a raw-boned young man, freckled and tanned. He stood awkwardly on one foot, and looked from one to the other of the four men who faced him. Inspector Bowes he knew, his expression seemed to say, but who on earth were these strangers?

"Now, Cartwright," said Shelley, "I understand that you come from Penistone?"

"Ay."

"That's your home, is it?"

"Ay."

"Lived there all your life?"

"Ay."

"So I suppose that you'll know pretty well everyone in the place, where they live, and so on."

"Ay."

Cartwright, Shelley told himself with an inward smile, was clearly a man of few words.

"Well, then, I want you to think and then answer me to the best of your ability," Shelley said, and again the young man said "Ay."

"Do you know a house or farm or something in or near Penistone the name of which begins with the word 'Black'?" asked Shelley.

There was dead silence for a few moments. They all looked at the awkward young man and waited for him to make up his mind about the matter. It seemed an endless time, while he stood awkwardly by, before he made up his mind, and found his tongue.

"Ay," he said. "I remember them, but which one would you want?"

"Which one? Is there more than one house of that name?" asked Shelley.

"Ay."

"What are they called?"

"There's Blackdown House, and there's Blackthorn Farm, and there's Black Horse Inn. That's three, anyhow."

"Should think we could cut out the inn, in any case," was Shelley's comment. "But what about the other two? Either of them strike a familiar chord in your memory, Mr. Fairhurst?"

Henry shook his head helplessly. "Not an atom of remembrance of either of them, Mr. Shelley," he admitted.

"Ah, well, that's one of the perils of a detective's job," said Shelley in playful ruefulness. "His best witness always seems to let him down at the moment when it is most necessary that he should not."

"But what do you propose to do?" asked Inspector Bowes.

"If you'll be so kind as to lend us this young man for an hour or two, I propose to have a look at both of the houses mentioned," Shelley explained. "I think it's pretty certain that we'll find Mr. Wallace in one of them."

"Certainly," answered the local man. "Cartwright, you'll go with Inspector Shelley and show him where the two houses are. Got that?"

"Ay, sir."

"And don't you dare to do anything foolish. Inspector Shelley has come from Scotland Yard, and the man you're helping him to catch is a murderer. Do you get that, Cartwright, my lad?"

"Ay, sir." There was not a movement in his impassive face, not a quiver of a muscle to show the excitement which young Constable Cartwright was feeling. To think, he told himself, that he was working with a man from Scotland Yard! And in a murder case, too!

"There's a car at your service, Mr. Shelley," Inspector Bowes told him. "It'll be round in a moment now. And the driver will take you to the door."

"Thanks, Inspector. Very decent of you," answered Shelley. "We don't always meet with such consideration from the local men we have to work with, I can assure you. And it's a real pleasure to meet a man who understands exactly what's wanted."

Without obviously flattering, Shelley always thought it worth while to keep in with the local men with whom he had to work. It made for better feelings, and for greater efficiency. He had known of Scotland Yard men who had failed because in a foolish manner they had antagonised the local police; and so had not been put into touch with some vital clue.

So he smiled gratefully at Inspector Bowes as they made their way towards the waiting car, and waved his hand to the local man as he stood on the step of the police station and watched them move slowly off across the rough, cobbled street.

It was a nightmare drive, and Shelley found himself comparing it with a previous occasion when he had been engaged on a similar chase across the dreary waste of Dartmoor. Now here he was engaged on a chase across another moor, some hundreds of miles farther north, and with, he hoped, a similarly successful conclusion ahead.

He found himself comparing the two scenes. Dartmoor, with its sudden outcrops of grey granite, its main colour purple and grey. Here the land was more dismal and yet no less fascinating. Its mixtures of brown and fawn were delightful to the eye. And Shelley sometimes had the eye of an artist.

He recalled that it was not far from here that the Brontë sisters had eaten their hearts out in a country parsonage, and he admitted that the gloom of *Wuthering Heights* was understandable in such an atmosphere of cruel, bitter rocks and hills.

He thought, too, of the strangeness of fate, that had led him from the British Museum, centre of civilisation, to the bitter waste of a Yorkshire moor, still more or less as it had been when primitive man hunted his prey, the road a mere pale ribbon stretching over the endless hills.

But he was brought up with a jerk. The car had stopped.

"Blackdown House, sir," explained Constable Cartwright, and Shelley smiled.

"Good," he said. "Now for dear Mr. Wallace." He opened the door of the car and alighted. Cunningham, Henry Fairhurst, and Constable Cartwright followed him. They stood in the road and looked up at the dreary bulk of grey stone that towered its three tall stories above them.

Chapter XX

At Blackdown House

Blackdown House was quite an imposing place. It was built plainly, of a dull grey stone, and it was much taller than the other houses in the street. They were dwarfed in comparison, even though they were far from being the "workmen's cottages" which were to be found in neighbouring streets.

Shelley looked up at it with some concern. He had brought an automatic pistol with him, but he did not want to use it if its use could possibly be avoided. Yet there was no getting away from the fact that the man they were after was a double murderer, who would not hesitate to kill again if he thought that his ends could best be achieved by such means.

Shelley pondered the problem for a moment with wrinkled brow. The others looked at him, eager to do something but waiting for a lead from him before they decided what that "something" could be.

"The straightforward way seems the best," said Shelley.

"Okay, sir," answered Cunningham, and marched to the door of Blackdown House. Seizing the gnarled old knocker with his right hand, he banged it resolutely two or three times, arousing resounding echoes in the old house. Then they all waited for the result.

There was no result. The house stared at them solemnly, as if defying them to do their worst. But there was certainly no reply.

"Who lives here, Cartwright?" asked Shelley. "Do you happen to know?"

"Ay."

"Well, who is it?"

"A fellow called Ramsbottom. He's lived here for years and years."

"Is he often away from home?"

Cartwright shook his head sadly. "Can't say as I've ever heard of him leaving Penistone in his life," he said.

Shelley was disappointed. He had hoped that this was their goal at last, but the outlook, which had been quite promising, suddenly took on a more sinister appearance. It might be that they were climbing up the wrong tree after all. He tried not to feel too pessimistic about the whole affair, but he tried in vain. Then—quite suddenly—another thought came into his mind.

"Has he got a beard?"' he asked.

"Ay," answered Cartwright, and Shelley's heart sang again.

"Try again, Cunningham," he ordered, and Cunningham obeyed. He gave a perfect fusillade of knocks, awaking all the nooks and corners of the place, until housewives in other houses down the street threw open doors and poked inquisitive noses out of bedroom windows to see what was amiss. Still there was no reply. The house might have been an abode of the dead.

"Once more," said Shelley grimly, and Cunningham willingly complied.

This time there was some response. Shelley was watching the mysterious house with great care, and he saw a flutter of a window-blind in one of the rooms in the top story. It was the merest movement, and to a less observant eye it would doubtless have passed unnoticed. Not so with Shelley. He missed nothing.

"There's someone in," he announced. "Watch that blind up there, Cunningham. There it goes again!" And certainly the blind had been lifted the smallest fraction of an inch, as if someone inside had endeavoured to peer out to see who was disturbing the peace of this still somnolent street.

"Bang again, Cunningham," he ordered, "and go on banging until there's some response. That's the only way that we shall get anywhere. Whoever he is, he's hiding himself away damned mysteriously. Still, I don't want to break the door down if I can possibly avoid it. After all, the man may be innocent. This may not be the place we're after, and we don't want to make fools of ourselves to that extent, do we?"

Cunningham seized the door-knocker in a resolute grip, took a deep breath, and hammered away unmercifully for a full half-minute. Then he paused for breath, took a grip of the knocker once more, and prepared to make another fiendish din. It was not often that one had a chance, in the middle of a difficult case, to "let off steam" in this manner, and Cunningham was firmly resolved to make the most of the opportunity while it lasted. But it was not to last much longer. Before he had a chance to start again on his banging activities, Shelley stopped him with a wave of an imperious hand.

"I think he's opening the window," he said. And, as usual, Shelley was right.

The window of the room in the top story, the room the window-blind of which they had previously seen quivering, slowly opened. They looked up, wondering what the result might be. A head looked out, and a quavering voice enquired: "What's all the row about down there?"

Shelley looked at the face that was disclosed to their view. At once he was compelled to admit that, unless this was the most brilliant of disguises, it could not be the man they were after.

The man who gazed down at them, his eyes screwed up in the difficult task of vision, was old, incredibly old. His face was a mass of wrinkles, and his beard was a dirty white. Shelley could not, from that distance below, see what the old man was clothed in, but what was visible appeared to be the collar of a very dirty old nightshirt.

Shelley cursed that he had not thought of asking Cartwright the colour of the old man's beard. Then he might have been prepared for this shock. Still, better late than never, so he turned to Cartwright with a somewhat sheepish grin.

"That Mr. Ramsbottom?" he asked quietly.

"Ay," answered Cartwright, and Shelley groaned. It looked as if they were on the wrong track after all, for certainly this old fogey was not the man they were after. Yet it was just barely possible that their enemy was hidden somewhere in the house, so they must make some sort of attempt to get in.

"We're the police," he shouted back. "Hunting an escaped prisoner."

"Eh?" The old man appeared to be rather deaf.

On Shelley repeating his request to find the escaped prisoner, however, the old man seemed to understand what they were getting at. At any rate he acquiesced, and promised to come down and let them in. Then he slammed down the window with a vicious bang, and they settled down, as patiently as possible, to another wait, which, truth to tell, seemed even longer than the previous one, for then they had the active interest of knocking and watching to see if the knock would draw forth any response.

Eventually, however, the old man opened the door to them, and, grumbling under his breath about people who came disturbing peace-loving citizens in the middle of the night, led the way indoors.

He was, as Shelley had surmised, dressed in a long nightshirt which might once have been cream-coloured with stripes of some darker colour, but which now, by dint of many washes at infrequent intervals, had turned into a kind of indeterminate grey.

"Now, what is it that you want, lads?" he asked as soon as they reached the sitting-room, which was crowded with the most incredible mixture of Victorian bric-à-brac. "Old junk," was Shelley's mental comment, but he was careful not to let his distaste become obvious.

He proceeded to explain: "There's a dangerous criminal escaped, sir," he said, "and we have reason to believe that he has sought refuge in your house. We want you to allow us to search the place, so that we can either catch him or else make sure that he isn't here."

"Eh, but that's bad news," was the old man's comment. "But how do you know that he's in this house?"

"We don't know for certain," Shelley explained patiently. "It's only a suspicion. But, you see, suspicion is generally about all we have to go on in our job."

The old man looked at them with an eye from which, in spite of his great age, all shrewdness had not yet departed, and then said: "But if there's a criminal in this house, lads, how do you reckon he got in? Answer me that."

"All sorts of ways," said Shelley, feeling decidedly uncomfortable, and suspecting that the old man was getting rather the best of this argument, and might well be merely talking and making futile objections in order to gain time and let the criminal escape. Still, they had left the constable who had driven the car standing in front of the house, and had sent Cartwright around to guard the back. So there should not be much doubt about that.

"What sorts of ways?" pursued Mr. Ramsbottom. "Give me just one instance, and then I'll try to tell you what I think about it all."

"There's the front door," Shelley began, but the old man quickly picked him up on that score. He cackled with unearthly glee.

"The front door I bolts and bars every night," he said. "And bolted and barred it was when I came down just a few minutes ago to let you lads in. So you can make up your mind about that, Mr. Policeman. No burglar came into this house by the front door, last night or any other night."

"Right," answered Shelley briskly, cursing himself that he had suggested such a ridiculous thing. "Well, what about the back door? I suppose that a house of this size must have a back door somewhere."

The old man cackled again. "Locked likewise," he said. "I had a look at it, just to make sure, before I let you in just now."

"Well, windows, then," suggested Shelley in desperation. "There are so many ways in which he might have got in that 'twould be quicker if you would allow us to have a quick glance around than if we went through all the possibilities with you."

"All right, then," said Mr. Ramsbottom. "If you want to have a squint around you shall. But don't expect me to come with you. I should catch me death of cold if I went all over this old barn of a house in my nightshirt."

"That's all right, Mr. Ramsbottom," said Shelley with some relief. "We shall be all right. Only one thing, though: is there anyone else in the house? We don't want to go wandering into somebody's bedroom, and giving them a dreadful fright."

Again that crazy cackle burst upon their ears.

"Eh, that's all right, lads," said Ramsbottom. "There's nobody in the house barring myself. I've lived here all alone for nigh on twenty years, and I reckon that I shall go on living here alone until I die."

"Right," said Shelley, and then proceeded to split up their little party.

"You take the ground floor, Cunningham," he said, "and keep Mr. Fairhurst with you."

Henry had been strangely quiet during all the discussion, but at this he plainly jibbed.

"Mr. Shelley," he said, "I think that I should be allowed to come with you."

"Mr. Fairhurst," answered Shelley sternly, "you will do what you are told. It's bad enough having an outsider with us at all when we're engaged on chasing such a dangerous man as this, but the least that I can do is see that you are, as far as is possible, kept out of danger."

"But, Mr. Shelley—" Henry started to protest, but Shelley silenced him with a peremptory gesture.

"Another word, Mr. Fairhurst, and I shall tell you to go outside this house," he said. "I've had quite enough argument in this case already. From now on I manage it in my own way."

Henry shrugged his shoulders in mute acquiescence. There was, it seemed, nothing else to be said. Shelley had a forceful personality, and when he chose to assert himself in this way, no one—least of all, the meek and mild little Henry Fairhurst—dared to offer him any sustained opposition.

"I'm going upstairs," Shelley announced. "If I fire this"— he held up the automatic—"I want you, Cunningham, to come upstairs as quickly as you can. It will mean that I have the man cornered."

"What do I do?" asked Henry plaintively.

"You, Mr. Fairhurst," announced Shelley, "stay here whatever happens. I hope that I have made that perfectly clear— *whatever happens*. Do you understand exactly what I mean?"

"Yes," said Henry, and sighed deeply. It seemed, in spite of his ambition to become a real detective, that he was to be kept out of the way when anything really exciting was happening.

"Right," said Shelley. "I hope that's all clear. Wish me good hunting, Cunningham. We'll have Mr. Wallace under lock and key before very long."

"Good luck, sir," said Cunningham, and Shelley, his automatic firmly gripped in his right hand, made his way to the staircase, which branched off the back of the entrance hall of the house.

At the top of the first flight of stairs he paused. A long corridor ran the length of the house, and there were half a dozen doors off it, any one of which might be hiding the killer. It was a ticklish job chasing a man in these conditions, but Shelley had undertaken many ticklish jobs in his time, and he was quite prepared to do his best with this one.

He opened the first door, to see an empty room, bare boards, shabby, broken walls, and a dirty ceiling. Obviously Mr. Ramsbottom, living alone in this great barracks of a house, did not attempt to use it all or to furnish all the rooms. He clearly preferred to live in a few rooms, leaving the others in this empty, untidy, dirty state.

Still, it simplified Shelley's task. Three of the six rooms on that floor were completely uninhabited in this fashion, their gloomy emptiness adding to the uncanny effect which the house seemed to be having on Shelley's mind. At no time a very sensitive man, Shelley found himself shivering as his feet woke ancient echoes on the rough boards of the third room. How many more rooms like this was he to find?

The others were different, however. The first was a bedroom—or rather, it had been a bedroom at some time in the more or less remote past. The bed, the dressing-table, the old-fashioned wash-stand, were all draped in ghost-like dust-sheets. Spiders' webs descended from the corners of the richly ornamented ceilings. The place could not have been lived in for years.

And the same applied to the next two rooms. One had once been a billiard-room, but the cushions of the ancient billiard-table were hard as bricks. The third was a drawing-room of some sort, but here again there was the same dead atmosphere.

Shivering in spite of himself, Shelley came out of the last room, retraced his footsteps to the head of the stairs, and shouted down.

"Any luck, Cunningham?" He knew what the answer would be before it came up to him in Cunningham's stentorian voice from the floor below.

"No, sir, not a trace of a soul anywhere. I think we're on the wrong track."

"I think so too," Shelley answered. "There's no one on the first floor. Still, I must have a look at the floor above, just to make sure."

"Right-ho, sir," answered Cunningham cheerfully. "I'll just hang on down here."

"I don't expect that I shall keep you very long," said Shelley.

And he was right. The top floor was more or less a repetition of the previous one, except that there were two rooms which had been lived in—the bedroom from which old Mr. Ramsbottom had first looked down at them, and another room, which was apparently drawing-room, dining-room, and kitchen all rolled into one.

But any trace of an inhabitant apart from Mr. Ramsbottom himself Shelley could not find anywhere in the house. It was all very disheartening, but it was not the first time that Shelley had been led astray by a false clue, and he walked down the stairs in a fairly good temper. It was, after all, quite possible that the criminal was at the other place which Cartwright had mentioned—Blackthorn Farm was it?—and that was quite clearly indicated as their next port of call.

"No go, Mr. Ramsbottom," Shelley told the old man as he reached the ground floor. "Must have been a false alarm after all, I think. We shall have to look for our criminal else-where."

For the last time the old man emitted his uncanny cackle. "I never thought you'd find him here, my lad," he said.

"Why not?" asked Shelley, as he made his way to the front door.

"Because everybody in Penistone knows that old Jim Ramsbottom's got no brass," the old man explained. "And what yon criminals are after is brass, every time."

"That's true in most cases, Mr. Ramsbottom," Shelley admitted, "but not in this case."

"No?"

"No. You see, this man was running away from the police. And a man who's running away from the police will go anywhere where he thinks he's likely to be safe."

"Ay. That's so," the old man agreed.

"Well, folks," said Shelley, as they settled themselves once more in the police car. "I guess we now try our luck at Blackthorn Farm."

"Ay," returned Cartwright.

"Where is it?" asked Shelley.

"Matter of two or three miles outside the town," Cartwright explained.

"Matter of five or six minutes, then," said Shelley with a smile; and settled down to enjoy the scenery.

Chapter XXI

The Hunt Is Up

Violet awoke from a deep sleep which had been disturbed by the most absurd and ridiculous dreams. Her face expressed the most complete bewilderment, as one who says: "What am I doing here, and where is it anyway?" Then, suddenly, memory came back; there flowed into her mind a thought of her dreadful plight, and she had to fight hard to keep back the tears that sprang unbidden to her eyes.

Above her loomed the bearded figure of her captor. He grasped her shoulder roughly in a large hand, and had obviously shaken her into waking.

"You must get up," he muttered viciously.

"Why?" Violet was still half asleep, and she rubbed her eyes like a child just getting out of bed on a cold morning.

"It is necessary," he said, speaking slowly and deliberately, almost as if explaining something very difficult and complicated to the child that she appeared to be, "that we should leave this house at once."

"But I don't want to leave," Violet objected. "I am very comfortable where I am, thank you."

"You will do as I tell you," he said roughly. "It is enough that I tell you that we leave this house at once. I order you, and you obey. It is only on that agreement that we can proceed at all. Do you understand what I am saying to you?"

"I suppose so," Violet agreed. "In any case, as I seem to be quite helpless in your hands, I suppose I must do as you tell me."

He positively purred his satisfaction at this sudden change of front.

"Ah," he said, "that is better. That is much better, thank you, Miss Arnell. If you will just adopt a sensible attitude like that—ah, then we shall get somewhere. I might tell you that if you try to dispute my right to tell you what to do…" And he paused significantly.

"What will you do?" Violet's question sounded quite innocent; but actually she was playing for time, realising that this decision on his part must be an indication that the pursuit was near at hand.

"What will I do?" He laughed harshly in tones that grated unpleasantly on her ear. "I will proceed, my dear Miss Arnell, to give you a little injection with a delightful little drug which I have in my possession. That drug will ensure that you will take no interest in the proceedings for—oh, for a considerable time." Again that harsh laugh rang out; and Violet found herself, in spite of her steely determination not to flinch, to show no fear of this evil man, shuddering at the dreadful menace of his tones. He positively exuded evil, as if he were the personification of evil himself.

"So you see," he was going on, "it will be as well for you to do as I tell you. Such behaviour will be more sensible and will mean less trouble for all concerned, including yourself— I said, including your dear self, my dear young lady."

Violet thought that he was more detestable when he tried to be pleasant than when he was in his determinedly commanding moods; but she made no objections, and suffered herself to be led from the room down the stairs and out of the front door of the house. Here she found the car waiting, and she was bundled into it. Rapidly the man drove off. At the end of what was apparently a private road he alighted, opened a farm gate which straddled the entrance to the main road, and then returned to the car. He drove off again.

As they went along the road Violet found herself glancing around her, looking to try to get her bearings, so to speak, in this strange country where she had been a prisoner for some time. She could not imagine how long she had been here, for she might have slept for an hour or a day; nor did she know how long she had been unconscious in the house prior to her first awakening.

She saw a stretch of broad moorland, dotted here and there with grey outcrops of granite, and with dirty-looking sheep grazing here and there on the rugged slopes of cruel hills. On one occasion her captor swerved to avoid one of these sheep, muttered a curse, and swerved back on to the road once more, having gone within inches of a drop which must have been several hundred feet. Violet drew a deep breath of relief when she saw the ribbon of road winding its brown length ahead of them again. Her captor merely chuckled as he glanced at her white face.

"Narrow shave, eh?" he said. "Trust me. I'm a good driver, I am. Never had a smash yet, nor a serious breakdown that I couldn't remedy. You're in safe hands when you're in a car with me, my dear."

Almost as if to disprove his words, the car slowed down, the engine uttering uncouth sounds, and then stopped abruptly in the middle of the road.

"Hell!" muttered the man, pressing the self-starter energetically. It emitted loud buzzes, but the car still remained quite stationary.

"Looks as if this is the occasion where your ability falls down flat, Mr. Man," announced Violet with a cheeky grin, her confidence returning.

"Not a bit of it," he replied. "I'll soon put this right." He rose from his seat, and, carefully locking the doors of the car on the outside and pocketing the keys, made his way to the front, where he threw open the bonnet and gazed at the engine for a few minutes.

He tinkered with the engine ineffectively for some time, then came round to the side again, unlocking the door and motioning her to get out and join him.

"What's the meaning of all this?" she asked.

"Never you mind," he grunted, and grasped her wrist tightly, dragging her out of the car by main force and landing her, breathless, in the road.

"Look here," she protested. "What on earth does all this mean, sir? You drag me all over the country, and then you land me on a God-forsaken moor in the middle of Yorkshire—if what you tell me is true—and now apparently you expect me to tramp all over the north of England with you. I tell you, whatever power you have, this is just not good enough."

"Don't be a fool, my dear," he said—a little more pleasantly, it is true. "We're only walking as far as the nearest garage."

"How far is that?"

"How the hell should I know?"

"Well, I'm not going to walk ten miles with you."

"You're going to walk a hundred miles if I tell you to," he answered roughly. "That car won't run without petrol, and to get some petrol we must get to a garage."

Violet laughed. "So the all-efficient kidnapper forgot to fill up his petrol-tank!" she chaffed him, almost forgetting, in her amusement at this puerile slip, the peril in which she stood at that moment.

"Yes," he said. "And, since I can't leave you in the car until I come back, I have to take you to the nearest garage with me. And if you don't do as I tell you—well, I warn you that I have other methods. I can force you to do exactly what I wish. So don't try to disobey me, or it will be the worse for you. Understand?" He pulled his hand out of his overcoat pocket, to reveal the fact that it held an enormous, villainous-looking revolver, and Violet, this time, had no difficulty in reminding herself that this man was probably a murderer.

They tramped along the road, the man's hand tightly gripped on her arm, and Violet looked at the cruel hill above her, and the dangerous precipice below, wondering if an attempt to escape would be possible. Then she decided that it would not. This man, who was no doubt an excellent shot with a revolver, would be able to pick her off without difficulty long before she got out of revolver-shot. So the only thing to do was to carry on, and hope that some opportunity to escape might offer itself later. So she obediently altered her pace to fit her captor's pace as he strode hurriedly along the road.

As the car sped out of Penistone Shelley kept his eyes anxiously bent on the road ahead.

"How far did you say?" he asked.

"Two or three miles," answered Cartwright.

"Shan't be long, then," said Shelley in composed tones, but Cunningham knew well enough that his chief was feeling the most intense excitement. That look of intense concentration, the steel-grey eyes fixedly following the road that wound its way up the hill ahead of them, was unmistakable.

They followed a road that was now rapidly running into open moorland. Shelley noticed, as Violet had noticed before him, the curious blend of brown in the hills, the granite that projected at their tops, the sheep of an indeterminate dirty colour that were dotted here and there on the perilous slopes of the hills, clinging precariously at points where it would have seemed totally impossible for any animal to secure satisfactory foothold.

"Wait!" exclaimed Cartwright as they passed a gate off the main road. "Yon's the place."

The driver obediently stopped the car, and swivelled round in his seat.

"Where? Through that gate?" he asked.

"Ay," answered Cartwright. "Couple of hundred yards up there. 'Tis a big farmhouse, you know."

While this explanation was being made the deft driver had reversed the car and reached the gate.

"Hullo," remarked Cartwright. "That's queer."

"What's queer?" Shelley was, as always, eager to discover any strange things that were happening, for he knew that any which might crop up in any case would probably prove to be valuable clues. Such, at any rate, had been his experience in the past; and such, he was firmly convinced, was to be his destiny in the future.

Cartwright frowned in a puzzled manner. "Never before," he announced, "have I seen the gate open."

"How did they get out, then?" asked Cunningham.

"I don't exactly mean that," Cartwright said with a somewhat sheepish grin. "I mean that never before have I seen the gate left open. When anybody came in or out they always shut the gate behind them."

"H'm." Shelley looked thoughtful. "Probably the birds have flown, then. Wonder how they got wind of it?"

Cunningham had a suggestion to offer. "You remember," he said, "how, when we left Penistone, we came to the top of a high hill?"

Shelley nodded.

"Well," his assistant went on, "if a man at the top of this house"—he pointed to the farmhouse which they were now rapidly approaching—"had a telescope and watched the road, as he might if he suspected that he was being followed, he would see us there, a mile or more away, and would be able to get out of the place long before we got near enough to see *him*."

"Yes," Shelley agreed. "And we should be in the valley below, so that we should know nothing whatever about it. I fear very much that something like that has happened, and that we have a bit more chasing to do before the affair is finished, and before the present identity of our friend Mr. Wallace is revealed to us."

"We shall soon see," remarked Cunningham.

"Yes," said Shelley.

And they did see. They had now arrived at the house, which looked deserted enough in all conscience. The front door was wide open, as if left carelessly by fleeing inhabitants. Yet, when they cautiously proceeded into the house itself it showed every sign of recent occupation. On the table in the little breakfast-room off the roomy kitchen a meal was laid on the table. An egg had been eaten, its shell in an egg-cup remaining on the table. Shelley went over to the table and grasped the metal coffee-pot which rested on a cork mat on the polished oak table.

"We're mighty close on their trail, Cunningham," he said with a satisfied grin.

"How do you know?" asked Cunningham.

"Feel this coffee-pot."

Cunningham touched it gingerly, and then whistled. "Hot!" he exclaimed.

"Yes; we've missed them by about ten minutes at the most," said Shelley.

They hurried upstairs and looked around the various rooms of the house. Few showed any signs of recent habitation, but there was, as Cunningham had suggested, a telescope in one of the bedrooms. It was facing a window, and Shelley applied his eye to its lens. Then he too whistled, a shrill, almost uncanny note.

"Cunningham," he said, "I think I shall have to suggest that you get some promotion."

"Why? Was I right?"

"You were. Dead right. This telescope is turned to face that spot on the hill that you spoke about. It is focussed exactly for the spot. Quick! We must look around the other rooms, and then be off after them."

In a bedroom, however, they found something that detained them for a moment. Henry Fairhurst, who had been strangely quiet for some time, pounced on a handbag which was lying on the floor.

"That's Miss Arnell's!" he shouted with some excitement.

Shelley picked it up, opened it, and glanced at its muddled contents.

"Quite right, Mr. Fairhurst," he admitted. "Well, that clinches the whole affair. Mr. Wallace has Miss Arnell here in Yorkshire. And they can't be very far away, judging by the heat of the coffee in the pot on the breakfast-table downstairs."

"How are you going to catch them?" asked Henry.

"Watch me and see," answered Shelley. He ran down the stairs, the others following him helter-skelter.

Out of the front door Shelley ran; Cunningham, who was a burly man, puffed in his wake, and the others straggled along in the rear.

Shelley paused in front of the house, anxiously scanning the gravel, which was loosely thrown on the little private road which led from the main road up to the house itself, and up which they had driven a mere few minutes earlier.

"Ah!" he exclaimed at length. "Here we are. See, Cunningham?"

Henry Fairhurst peered at the two detectives, as they looked at the ground.

"Yes," said Cunningham. "An old Dunlop with a patch. That should be easy enough to follow."

"Good," answered Shelley. "In the car, quickly, gentlemen, if you don't mind. We're close to them now, and we shall soon have them."

Soon they were in the car, and Shelley gave his instructions to the driver. "Drive down to the main road as fast as you can," he said, "and then stop at the gate."

The driver complied readily enough, and soon they were at the gate once more. Shelley and Cunningham descended from the car, and examined the road very carefully. At first they did not seem to agree. There was a good deal of head-shaking and discussion. Soon, however, they reached a decision.

"Turn right," Shelley told the driver as they got back into the car. "Then drive hell-for-leather until we catch them. Don't care about speed limits; they don't matter in this case."

As they swung out into the road, the car took up speed and then raced along the road, the speedometer quivering higher and higher on its dial. Henry Fairhurst held his breath with suppressed excitement. This, he told himself, was the real thing. Sarah would have to believe him now. Never again would she be able to order him about, see that he wore bed-socks and took his aspirin when an influenza epidemic was on. He had been in on the end of a man-hunt, and no one, after this, would be able to order him about any more.

Chapter XXII

The End of the Chase

"You think then, sir," said Cunningham as they rolled along the road, "that this man who has kidnapped Miss Arnell is the murderer?"

"Not a doubt about it," answered Shelley absent-mindedly, his whole attention being concentrated on the road ahead.

"But why?" Cunningham persisted.

"Why what?"

"Why did he kill those two men?"

"My dear Cunningham, your memory is failing you," laughed Shelley. "Because he forged the will, and then killed Arnell, under the impression that the two men whose signatures as witnesses he had forged were both dead. When he found that one of them was still alive, he had to be killed in his turn. And that, as in all these double murder cases, was where he slipped up so badly. If he had been content with the murder of Arnell he would probably have got away with it quite satisfactorily. Baker would have been arrested, and tried, and hanged. And everyone would have been satisfied."

"Except Baker, of course," added Henry Fairhurst in a voice that was so faint as to be almost a whisper.

Shelley laughingly agreed. But it seemed that Cunningham was in a persistent mood, for he went on with his questioning, casting only the merest occasional glance at the road ahead. After all, it was just as well to get everything clear before the final scene of the mystery, which, he thought, would probably be very like the final scene in other mysteries in which he had been concerned. After all the excitement of a murder-hunt, it always seemed to Cunningham that the mere prosaic fact of an arrest came as an anticlimax. Still, he told himself (and here Henry Fairhurst would certainly have agreed with him) this case was in one respect unique. They were chasing an undoubted murderer. He had a known identity as a criminal with a record. Yet they did not know his motive in the case, nor did they know who he was. That he must be someone with whom they had already come into contact in the case was certain.

"Who do you think he is?" he asked, as this train of thought started in his mind.

"Who do I think who is?" asked Shelley, who seemed to have somehow developed a most irritating strain of repeating each question as it was put to him.

"The murderer."

"J. K. Wallace."

"But who is J. K. Wallace?"

"Con-man and general swindler."

"I know that, chief. But what's he doing in this case?"

"That," Shelley announced, "is just what I should like to know, Cunningham. I'm pretty certain that the motive will stare us in the face when we know how he's connected with Moses Moss. It's pretty obvious that he must have some sort of hold over that young man."

"Blackmail," Cunningham suggested.

"I rather fancy not," was Shelley's comment. "You see, I've made some enquiries into that young man's past history, and, while he's never done much honest hard work, yet he's never, as far as I can find out, been on the shady side of the law. He's always had enough sense to run straight—at any rate, as far as I've been able to find out. Of course, there may have been some hidden transactions in the past which we haven't been able to trace."

"Mr. Shelley," interposed Henry Fairhurst unexpectedly.

"Yes." Shelley turned round and faced the little man, whose face was positively shining with the excitement of the information which had, it appeared, suddenly occurred to him.

"I suppose it never occurred to you to find out if Mr. Moss had any ability as an artist."

"You think he might have forged the will himself, I suppose," commented Shelley.

"The thought did occur to me," Henry admitted, and his beam grew brighter than ever. But it was a beam which was soon quenched.

"We did enquire about that," Shelley said. "And he had no artistic ability at all, as far as was known."

Henry's face fell.

"Then you think that he had nothing to do with it," he said.

"I wouldn't go as far as to say that," answered Shelley. "But I should be prepared to take a bet of ten to one that he knows nothing about the murders."

"H'm." Henry did not seem at all impressed, but did not feel inclined to dispute the issue. And, in any case, further argument was prevented by a sudden discovery of Shelley.

"Stop!" he shouted, and, with a shriek of protest from the brakes, the obedient driver brought the speeding car to a sudden standstill.

"What's the matter?" asked Cunningham in puzzled tones; and Shelley pointed to a stationary car which was just in front of them. It was a fast-looking, rakish sports saloon.

"What price Mr. Wallace?" Shelley murmured, and Cunningham, not for the first time in his career, marvelled at his chief's wonderful powers of observation, able to pay attention to every vehicle on the road at the same time as he was carrying on a conversation which would have occupied the whole mind of most people.

"Looks like it, doesn't it?" he said; and then followed Shelley on to the road and over to the empty car.

They looked at the tyres, and then Shelley gave vent to a grunt of pleased satisfaction.

"See," he said, and pointed to the back off wheel. Cunningham obediently looked, and at once saw the cause of Shelley's satisfaction. The tyre was a Dunlop, and it had a patch. This was certainly the car that had driven out of Blackthorn Farm, just prior to their arrival at the deserted house!

"Cunningham," said Shelley, emotion making his voice tremble. "Cunningham, my lad, we've got him!"

"Why did he abandon the car, I wonder?" Cunningham murmured.

"Breakdown, I expect," answered Shelley, as he strode to the front of the car, threw open the bonnet, and made a cursory examination of the engine.

"Well, that was a bit of luck for us, anyhow," he said, pointing to the petrol-tank, from which he had just removed the cap.

"Ran out of petrol, eh?" said Cunningham, and roared with laughter.

"That's about it," answered Shelley. "And not so long ago, either," he added, feeling the radiator with his hand. "The radiator is still distinctly warm to the touch."

They hurriedly clambered back into the car, and were soon buzzing along the road again. By this time they had got well up into the hills, and the road twisted and turned almost like a corkscrew. Not far ahead they could see, in a dip of the hills, a stretch of grey mirror—one of the mighty reservoirs which keeps Sheffield supplied with water.

"Should catch him very soon," Shelley remarked. "He can't have got more than a mile or so." He leaned over the front seat in his excitement, as he gave further instructions to the driver.

"If you see a man and a girl walking," he said, "slow down, but not too much. We don't want to give him the alarm too soon, you know."

"That him, sir?" asked the driver, pointing to a steep hill ahead of them. Near its summit could be seen two human figures, easily recognisable, even at this distance, as a man and a girl.

"I believe it is," answered Shelley. He was quivering with excitement now, for he felt that the end of the long chase was at hand, and his excitement was in some subtle way communicated to the others.

Slowly they drew near to the two people ahead, and they realised that they were those whom they had been chasing. Suddenly, however, the man glanced over his shoulder, a look of anxiety and fear overspread his face, and he broke into a kind of shambling trot, the girl's arm tightly clasped in his hand.

"Drop that girl's arm, Wallace," Shelley shouted as they came within hearing distance. "We've got you!"

The man looked around once more, and then, dropping Violet's arm, he raced to the side of the road, vaulted the low stone hedge which separated it from the moorland, wild and dreary, and hurried up the steep slope of the hill.

Shelley opened the door of the car. "Look after the girl, Cunningham," he said. "I'm going after him." He took his automatic from his pocket, and vaulted the hedge in his turn.

But Wallace had got a considerable start on him, and the slope was steep. When Shelley reached the summit of the first little hill, Wallace was nowhere to be seen. Cautiously, the detective put his head around a large rock mass, only to draw it backwards quickly as a bullet whizzed by, unpleasantly near his ear.

"Ah-ha!" An insane, cackling laugh rang out. "You'll never catch me, Mr. Detective."

"Wallace," Shelley said sternly. "You know that you're beaten. You know that you'll never get out of these hills alive. Better give yourself up, my man."

The answer was another bullet and another laugh. "So I shan't get out of these hills alive, eh?" came the question, uncannily sounding from a man who was still hidden securely behind another rock, not far from the edge of what appeared to Shelley to be a steep, precipitous drop, the reservoir's still depths being far below the level at which they had arrived.

"Well," the owner of the voice went on, "if I don't get out alive, neither shall you, my fine fellow."

"What's the use," asked Shelley, gripping his automatic tightly, and wondering if there was some way in cutting off his adversary's retreat, "of trying to kill me? It won't make things any better for you. You've killed two men already."

"Yes," came the answer. "I've killed two men already, and I'll kill more before I've done. They can only hang me once, no matter how many men I've killed." And again there sounded that wild laughter, echoing in the hills so that it seemed to Shelley as if the whole atmosphere was quaking with crazy mirth.

Then Shelley saw the man's head. He was slowly peering around the corner of the rock behind which he had contrived to hide himself. Shelley drew his automatic, took quick aim, and fired. He saw a piece of rock close by the man's head detach itself from the bulk of the granite. But the head was rapidly withdrawn.

"You'll have to shoot better than that, Mr. Detective," said the man, but Shelley felt that there was a little uncertainty in his tone now. No longer was there any of that laughter in his voice. It betrayed anxiety and fear.

Then the end came—it came far more quickly than Shelley had anticipated. He was watching the man carefully—or rather, he was watching the rock behind which the man was still hiding. Suddenly Wallace emerged. His face was deathly pale, and his beard stood out very black against the clear whiteness of his skin.

"Come on, damn you!" he shouted, waving a revolver around his head, and walking backwards away from the rock. "Come on and fight! If you can hit me, I'll give in. If I can hit you, you'll have to let me go free. How's that for a bargain, my friend?"

Shelley replied: "A detective makes no bargain with a criminal, Wallace. You must give yourself up. Throw away that revolver, and come over here."

"Not me," said the man with a crafty grin. "You're afraid of me, that's what it is. You know what a good shot I am."

Suddenly Shelley sprang out from his shelter, as he saw what was happening. The man raised his revolver, taking a further step backward to prepare his aim, and…Shelley dashed towards him, but too late.

When he reached the spot where Wallace had been standing, he saw that the man's body was bouncing over and over down the precipitous slope on the very edge of which he had been standing. As he watched, Shelley perceived it fall with a resounding splash into the waters of the reservoir far below.

"So," said Shelley, "may perish all bad men."

Chapter XXIII

Some Documents

1. Extract from Report of Inspector Shelley to the Chief Commissioner of Police at New Scotland Yard.

The body of the guilty man was afterwards recovered from the reservoir. On it there were found documents (enclosed) showing that he had for some years been lending money to Moses Moss, having been told by Moss that he had a rich uncle—Professor Arnell—who was in bad health, and who was going to leave him money. There is no evidence that Wallace ever believed this, but it seems probable that he soon formed his plot of murdering Professor Arnell and forging his will, thus ensuring that the money would be paid to him. He has been connected with several blackmail plots, and it is highly probable that he would later have blackmailed Moss, by pretending to have knowledge proving that Moss had killed his uncle.

He did not leave the money to Moss himself in the forged will because he was afraid that Moss would be suspected of the crime, and he knew that the will would be called invalid in that case.

He kidnapped Miss Arnell with the idea of terrorising her into marrying Moss, when the money would have come within his grasp. If she persisted in her refusal, he was planning to murder her also, but in such a way that it would merely seem that she had disappeared, and then the legal steps necessary to assuming her death would have been taken.

I may say that I am pleased that the man died in the way he did, for I am firmly convinced that if he had lived, we should have found that he was insane, and unfit to plead.

The way that things have turned out seem to me to be the better for all concerned.

(Signed) Henry Shelley, Detective-Inspector, C.I.D.

2. Letter from Henry Fairhurst to Moses Moss.

My dear Mr. Moss,

It was without doubt a most extraordinary concatenation of circumstances. But the fact remains, as I told you the other day, that the man who kidnapped our fair young friend wished her to enter into matrimony with yourself. And the other fact, which I promised that I would reveal to you as soon as circumstances rendered it in any way possible for me to do so, is merely this: the murderer and kidnapper of Miss Arnell, and the villain, in short, who was responsible for the troublous circumstances which have involved us all—and a strangely variegated crowd we were—was a man to whom you owed a lot of money. That was the item of evidence, so I am led to understand by our good friends the police, which first put them firmly on the somewhat difficult trail of the gentleman in question. I hope that you will follow me, my dear Mr. Moss. I conclude, my dear sir, with all good wishes to yourself.

Yours very sincerely,

Henry Fairhurst.

3. Letter from Violet Arnell to Inspector Shelley.

Dear Inspector Shelley,

I cannot tell you how grateful I am to you for all you have done. I may say that Harry joins me in this, for he feels that if it had not been for your valuable assistance in this dreadful business, we should never have been united.

Again with all our thanks,

Yours sincerely,

Violet Arnell.

P.S.—We get married on Tuesday next.

4. Letter from Moses Moss to Inspector Shelley.

Dear Inspector Shelley,

Mr. Fairhurst tells me that you think the murderer of Professor Arnell was a man to whom I owed money. He also tells me that he was a criminal who had previously been in the hands of the police—a man, I understand, called Wallace. But I assure you that I have never known anyone called Wallace, not to mention owing him money. Could you explain this to me, or is the secret too deep and too official, and all that sort of thing?

Yours faithfully,

Moses Moss.

5. Letter from Inspector Shelley to Moses Moss.

Dear Mr. Moss,

I can't understand how you didn't tumble to all this without my having to tell you. Mr. Wallace, who had been in our hands before over a little matter of a cheque that was wrongly signed, and who had, in the last few years, been making a pretty little income by blackmail, was also a money-lender. He had many of the younger "smart set" in his clutches, and his money-lending activities gave him a very useful jumping-off ground for his blackmail plots.

Need I say more? Oh, I suppose I must give you the name under which he carried on his business. It was Victor Isaacs, and he had an office in Ludgate Hill. The funny thing is that at one stage I suspected you, and, in making enquiries into your financial status (if I may thus refer to what is, I suppose, a pretty delicate matter), I actually visited Isaacs's office. But he was out, and I saw a clerk. At that very moment Isaacs was kidnapping Miss Arnell. Still, least said, soonest mended, all's well that ends well, and so on. Good luck to you!

Yours,

Henry Shelley.

6. Telegram from Inspector Shelley to Mr. and Mrs. Baker, honeymooning in Cornwall.

Bless you Violet. Bless you Harry. From your fairy godmother.

7. Retort of Miss Sarah Fairhurst when Mr. Henry Fairhurst told her the truth about the murder.

Fiddlesticks!

To receive a free catalog of Poisoned Pen Press titles, please provide your name, address, and email address in one of the following ways:

Phone: 1-800-421-3976
Facsimile: 1-480-949-1707
Email: info@poisonedpenpress.com
Website: www.poisonedpenpress.com

Poisoned Pen Press
6962 E. First Ave. Ste 103
Scottsdale, AZ 85251

CPSIA information can be obtained at www.ICGtesting.com
Printed in the USA
BVOW08s1625091016

464567BV00003B/172/P